STORIES FOR YOUNG PEOPLE

O. HENRY

Titles in this series:

Leo Tolstoy

Mark Twain

O. Henry

Oscar Wilde

STORIES FOR YOUNG PEOPLE

O. HENRY

EDITED BY JOHN HOLLANDER

ILLUSTRATED BY MILES HYMAN

STERLING PUBLISHING CO., INC.

New York

For Juliette, Charlotte and Eliot
—M.H.

Yet once more, for Adam, Lucy, and Noah
—J.H.

BOOK DESIGN BY DEBORAH KERNER / DANCING BEARS

Library of Congress Cataloging-in-Publication Data

Henry, O., 1982–1910
O. Henry / edited by John Hollander ; illustrated by Miles Hyman.
p. cm. – (Stories for young people)
Includes index.
Contents: The gift of the Magi—Mammon and the archer—After twenty years—Two Thanksgiving Day gentlemen—The last leaf—A retrieved reformation—The pimiento pancakes.
ISBN 1-4027-0988-9
[1. Short stories, American. 2. Short stories.] I. Hollander, John. II. Hyman, Miles, ill. III. Title. IV. Series

PZ7. H3964Oah 2005
[Fic]—dc22

2005049954

10 9 8 7 6 5 4 3 2 1

Published by Sterling Publishing Co., Inc.
387 Park Avenue South, New York, NY 10016

Distributed in Canada by Sterling Publishing
c/o Canadian Manda Group, 165 Dufferin Street
Toronto, Ontario, Canada M6K 3H6
Distributed in Great Britain and Europe by Chris Lloyd at Orca Book Services, Stanley House, Fleets Lane, Poole BH15 3AJ, England
Distributed in Australia by Capricorn Link (Australia) Pty. Ltd.
P.O. Box 704, Windsor, NSW 2756, Australia

Printed in China

Sterling ISBN 1-4027-0988-9

CONTENTS

INTRODUCTION

WILLIAM SYDNEY PORTER, who wrote under the penname O. HENRY, was the very popular author of several hundred short stories about American life around the beginning of the twentieth century. He was born in Greensboro, North Carolina, in 1862, where his father was a doctor. His aunt, a school teacher, educated him, and as a child he read widely, both in the great novelists of the nineteenth century and in popular fiction for boys.

Porter went to work in his uncle's drugstore, but after several years he took the opportunity to move to Texas, partly for his health and partly to strike out on his own. He stayed with some family friends on a sheep ranch near the Rio Grande and got to know cowboys and ranch hands; later on, he would write of them and their world in many of his stories.

He moved to Austin, Texas, and worked as a draftsman in a government Land Office. Porter drew very well and enjoyed doing cartoons. In Austin he founded and ran a humorous weekly publication called *The Rolling Stone* and wrote a daily humor column for a Houston newspaper. He took a job as a teller in a badly run bank in Austin.

He was later indicted for having mismanaged some of the bank's funds. It is believed that he would have been acquitted, since he was not a thief, but he left the U.S. for Honduras in Central America.

He lived there until, his wife being gravely ill, he returned to Texas. He was convicted in Federal Court and spent a few years in prison in Ohio. There the humorous journalist became an original author, writing stories based on what he had known in Honduras, on the ranch, and from the lives of other prisoners. After he was released, he moved to Pittsburgh. Once he had published a number of stories, Porter moved again to New York City, where he stayed for the rest of his life.

O. Henry stories are often quite short. They generally appeared in newspapers and magazines—for two years, he published at least one every week. Although the style is often spiced with allusions to classical mythology and great literature of the past, and although the plots are full of coincidences, his renditions of the lives and speech of his characters—whether rich or poor, young or old, cowboys, salesgirls, cops or criminals—all come from realistic observation. Although it is this realism that has made his stories endure, O. Henry may be most famous for the unexpected and often very surprising endings of his stories, It is hard to imagine a story that does not conclude with some astonishing revelation or ironic twist

It was New York that he wrote of with such love and detail in his second book, *The Four Million* (the title refers to the population of the city at the beginning of the twentieth century) and in many stories in his subsequent collections. He is most celebrated for these tales of New York life, although his stories about the southwest, drawing on his memories of Texas, are excellent as well.

Five of the stories selected for this book are indeed about New York — the widely known "The Gift of the Magi," "Two Thanksgiving-Day Gentlemen," "The Last Leaf," "Mammon and the Archer," and "After Twenty Years." This last story makes an interesting pair with "A Retrieved Reformation," which takes place in the midwest. In both tales a policeman who is not really the central character makes a difficult decision; but in one case doing so gives him pleasure and in the other, he does so sadly. "The Pimienta Pancakes," the last story in this collection, is of the lives of cowpunchers and sheep herders. It takes place in the same part of Texas in which William Sydney Porter first arrived as a young man starting out on a new life which would eventually take him to New York City and to great fame.

A final note, on currency: When it comes to matters of money, the reader should remember how much the value of a specific sum has changed over the last hundred years in the United States: a dollar then would be worth over twenty today.

THE GIFT OF THE MAGI

1906

The magi were "wise men from the east," as the Gospel According to St. Matthew calls them. Led by a star, they came to Bethlehem bringing gifts to "the young child with Mary his mother... of gold, and frankincense, and myrrh." In modern times, these became thought of as the original Christmas presents. This story, perhaps O. Henry's most famous one, is a tale of Christmas in New York City in about 1905. But the point of its title only becomes clear at the end. O. Henry frequently finishes off his stories by revealing to the reader a surprising coincidence that resolves a problem of some kind. In "The Gift of the Magi," the surprise ending reveals what we call an irony: the characters (and the reader as well) suddenly learn something that, had they known it beforehand, would have changed what they had done. The ending here, as you will see, seems at first to produce a sad and unsettling situation. It is exactly what Jim and Della, the young husband and wife in the story, do out of love for each other and the effects that each of the gifts have upon the other one, that results in this irony. The last paragraph, however, also implies that something else that Della and Jim continue to give each other is more important than any gift.

ONE DOLLAR AND EIGHTY-SEVEN CENTS. THAT was all. And sixty cents of it was in pennies. Pennies saved one and two at a time by bulldozing the grocer and the vegetable man and the butcher until one's cheeks burned with the silent imputation of parsimony that such close dealing implied. Three times Della counted it. One dollar and eighty-seven cents. And the next day would be Christmas.

There was clearly nothing to do but flop down on the shabby little couch and howl. So Della did it. Which instigates the moral reflection that life is made up of sobs, sniffles, and smiles, with sniffles predominating.

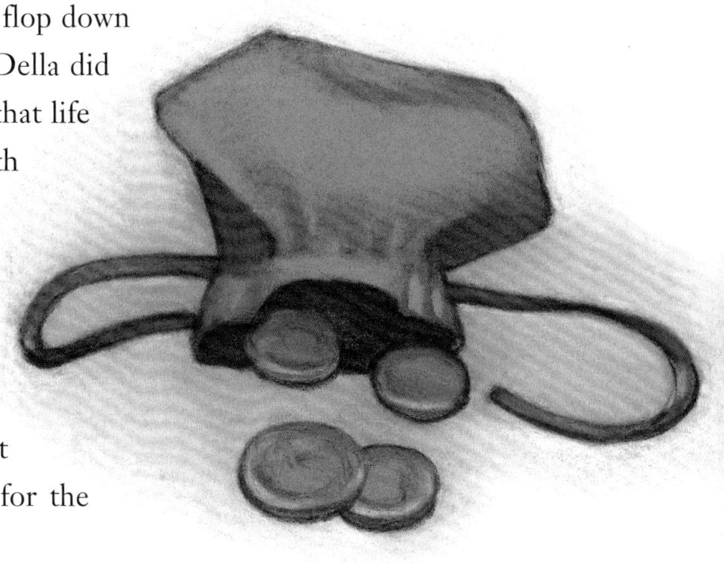

While the mistress of the home is gradually subsiding from the first stage to the second, take a look at the home. A furnished flat at eight dollars per week. It did not exactly beggar description, but it certainly had that word on the lookout for the mendicancy squad.

In the vestibule below was a letter-box into which no letter would go, and an electric button from which no mortal finger could coax a ring. Also appertaining thereunto was a card bearing the name "Mr. James Dillingham Young."

The "Dillingham" had been flung to the breeze during a former period of prosperity when its possessor was being paid thirty dollars per week. Now, when the income was shrunk to twenty dollars, though, they were thinking seriously of contracting to a modest and unassuming D. But whenever Mr. James Dillingham Young came home and reached his flat above he was called "Jim" and greatly hugged by Mrs. James Dillingham Young, already introduced to you as Della. Which is all very good.

imputation of parsimony—*accusation of cheapness*
instigates—*urges on*
beggar description—*was too elaborate to be described*
mendicancy squad—*police who arrest beggars*
appertaining thereunto—*having to do with that—this is legal language*

Della finished her cry and attended to her cheeks with the powder rag. She stood by the window and looked out dully at a gray cat walking a gray fence in a gray backyard. Tomorrow would be Christmas Day, and she had only one dollar and eighty-seven cents with which to buy Jim a present. She had been saving every penny she could for months, with this result. Twenty dollars a week doesn't go far. Expenses had been greater than she had calculated. They always are. Only one dollar and eighty-seven cents to buy a present for Jim. Her Jim. Many a happy hour she had spent planning for something nice for him. Something fine and rare and sterling—something just a little bit near to being worthy of the honor of being owned by Jim.

There was a pier-glass between the windows of the room. Perhaps you have seen a pier-glass in an eight-dollar flat. A very thin and very agile person may, by observing his reflection in a rapid sequence of longitudinal strips, obtain a fairly accurate conception of his looks. Della, being slender, had mastered the art.

Suddenly she whirled from the window and stood before the glass. Her eyes were shining brilliantly, but her face had lost its color within twenty seconds. Rapidly she pulled down her hair and let it fall to its full length.

Now, there were two possessions of the James Dillingham Youngs in which they both took a mighty pride. One was Jim's gold watch that had been his father's and his grandfather's. The other was Della's hair. Had the queen of Sheba lived in the flat across the airshaft, Della would have let her hair hang out the window someday to dry just to depreciate Her Majesty's jewels and gifts. Had King Solomon been the janitor, with all his treasures piled up in the basement, Jim would have pulled out his watch every time he passed, just to see him pluck at his beard from envy.

So now Della's beautiful hair fell about her rippling and shining like a cascade of brown waters. It reached below her knee and made itself almost a garment for her. And then she did it up again nervously and quickly.

sterling—*of the highest quality*
pier-glass—*tall, standing, framed mirror*
longitudinal—*vertical, lengthwise*
Sheba—*Arabian queen who visited King Solomon (I Kings, 10:1)*

Once she faltered for a minute and stood still while a tear or two splashed on the worn red carpet.

On went her old brown jacket; on went her old brown hat. With a whirl of skirts and with the brilliant sparkle still in her eyes, she fluttered out the door and down the stairs to the street.

Where she stopped the sign read: "Mne. Sofronie. Hair Goods of All Kinds." One flight up Della ran, and collected herself, panting. Madame, large, too white, chilly, hardly looked the "Sofronie."

"Will you buy my hair?" asked Della.

"I buy hair," said Madame. "Take yer hat off and let's have a sight at the looks of it."

Down rippled the brown cascade.

"Twenty dollars," said Madame, lifting the mass with a practiced hand.

"Give it to me quick," said Della.

Oh, and the next two hours tripped by on rosy wings. Forget the hashed metaphor. She was ransacking the store for Jim's present.

She found it at last. It surely had been made for Jim and no one else. There was no other like it in any of the stores, and she had turned all of them inside out. It was a platinum fob chain simple and chaste in design, properly proclaiming its value by substance alone and not by meretricious ornamentation—as all good things should do. It was even worthy of The Watch. As soon as she saw it she knew that it must be Jim's.

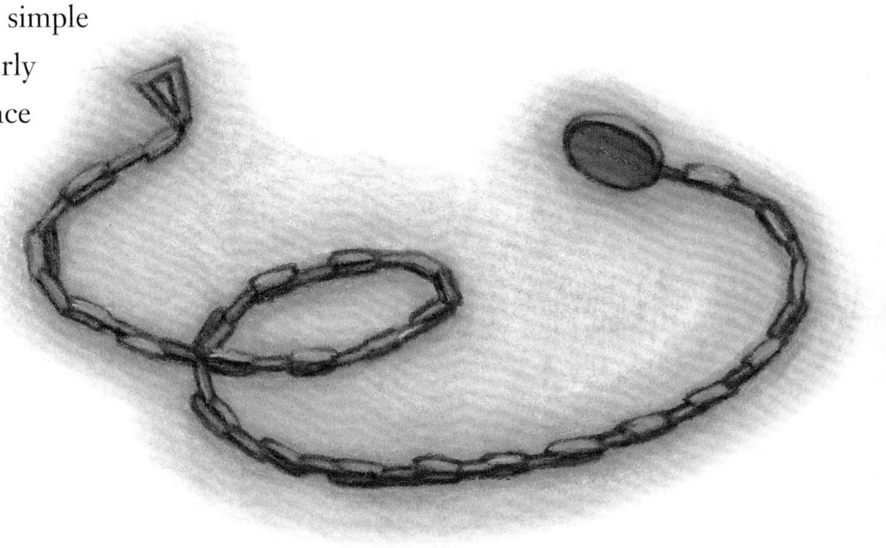

metaphor—*messed-up figure of speech*
platinum fob chain—*attached to a pocket watch and hanging outside a vest or pants watch-pocket; platinum is more expensive than gold*
meretricious—*attracting attention in a gross way*

It was like him. Quietness and value—the description applied to both. Twenty-one dollars they took from her for it, and she hurried home with the eighty-seven cents. With that chain on his watch Jim might be properly anxious about the time in any company. Grand as the watch was, he sometimes looked at it on the sly on account of the old leather strap that he used in place of a chain.

When Della reached home her intoxication gave way a little to prudence and reason. She got out her curling irons and lighted the gas and went to work repairing the ravages made by generosity added to love. Which is always a tremendous task, dear friends—a mammoth task.

Within forty minutes her head was covered with tiny, close-lying curls that made her look wonderfully like a truant schoolboy. She looked at her reflection in the mirror long, carefully, and critically.

"If Jim doesn't kill me," she said to herself, "before he takes a second look at me, he'll say I look like a Coney Island chorus girl. But what could I do—oh! what could I do with a dollar and eighty-seven cents?"

At seven o'clock the coffee was made and the frying-pan was on the back of the stove hot and ready to cook the chops.

Jim was never late. Della doubled the fob chain in her hand and sat on the corner of the table near the door that he always entered. Then she heard his step on the stair away down on the first flight, and she turned white for just a moment. She had a habit of saying a little silent prayer about the simplest everyday things, and now she whispered: "Please God, make him think I am still pretty."

The door opened and Jim stepped in and closed it. He looked thin and very serious. Poor fellow, he was only twenty-two—and to be burdened with a family! He needed a new overcoat and he was without gloves.

burdened with—*responsible for*

Jim stopped inside the door, as immovable as a setter at the scent of quail. His eyes were fixed upon Della, and there was an expression in them that she could not read, and it terrified her. It was not anger, nor surprise, nor disapproval, nor horror, nor any of the sentiments that she had been prepared for. He simply stared at her fixedly with that peculiar expression on his face.

Della wriggled off the table and went for him.

"Jim, darling," she cried, "don't look at me that way. I had my hair cut off and sold because I couldn't have lived through Christmas without giving you a present. It'll grow out again—you won't mind, will you? I just had to do it. My hair grows awfully fast. Say 'Merry Christmas!' Jim, and let's be happy. You don't know what a nice—what a beautiful, nice gift I've got for you."

"You've cut off your hair?" asked Jim, laboriously, as if he had not arrived at that patent fact yet even after the hardest mental labor. "Cut it off and sold it," said Della. "Don't you like me just as well, anyhow? I'm me without my hair, ain't I?"

Jim looked about the room curiously.

"You say your hair is gone?" he said, with an air almost of idiocy.

"You needn't look for it," said Della. "It's sold, I tell you—sold and gone, too. It's Christmas Eve, boy. Be good to me, for it went for you. Maybe the hairs of my head were numbered," she went on with sudden serious sweetness, "but nobody could ever count my love for you. Shall I put the chops on, Jim?"

Out of his trance Jim seemed quickly to wake. He enfolded his Della. For ten seconds let us regard with discreet scrutiny some inconsequential object in the other direction. Eight dollars a week or a million a year—what is the difference? A mathematician or a wit would give you the wrong answer. The magi brought valuable gifts, but that was not among them. This dark assertion will

setter—*bird-hunting dog*
patent—*obvious*
let us regard with discreet scrutiny some inconsequential object in the other direction.—*let's look away from the two of them embracing*
dark assertion—*puzzling statement*

be illuminated later on. Jim drew a package from his overcoat pocket and threw it upon the table.

"Don't make any mistake, Dell," he said, "about me. I don't think there's anything in the way of a haircut or a shave or a shampoo that could make me like my girl any less. But if you'll unwrap that package you may see why you had me going awhile at first."

White fingers and nimble tore at the string and paper. And then an ecstatic scream of joy; and then, alas! a quick feminine change to hysterical tears and wails, necessitating the immediate employment of all the comforting powers of the lord of the flat.

For there lay The Combs—the set of combs, side and back, that Della had worshipped long in a Broadway window. Beautiful combs, pure tortoise shell, with jeweled rims—just the shade to wear in the beautiful vanished hair. They were expensive combs, she knew, and her heart had simply craved and yearned over them without the least hope of possession. And now, they were hers, but the tresses that should have adorned the coveted adornments were gone.

But she hugged them to her bosom, and at length she was able to look up with dim eyes and a smile and say: "My hair grows so fast, Jim!"

And then Della leaped up like a little singed cat and cried, "Oh, oh!"

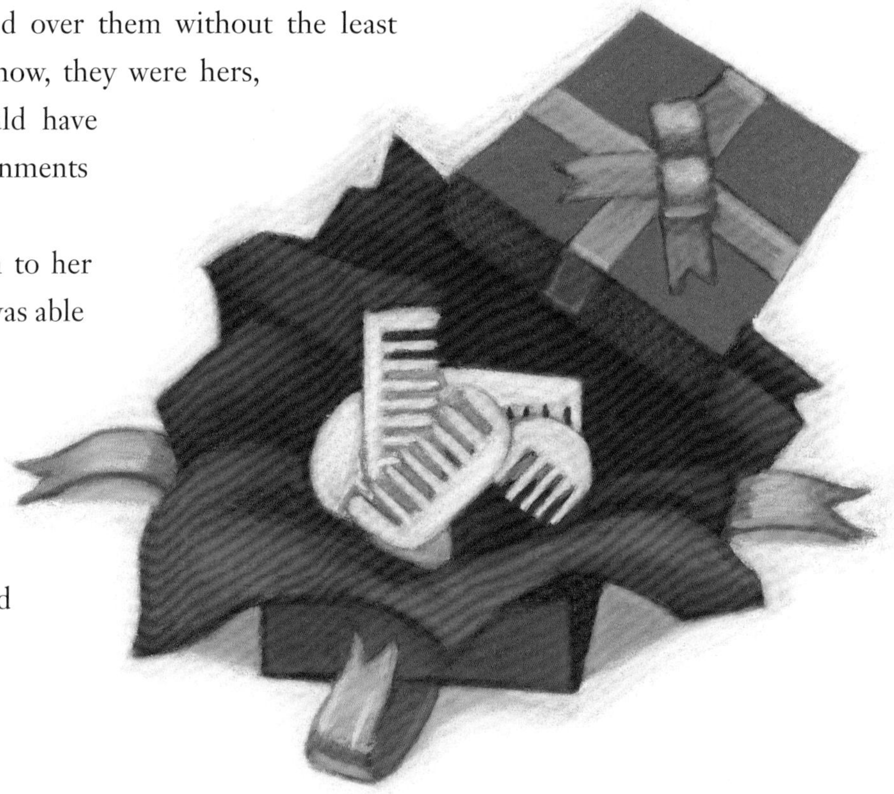

later on—*at the end of the story*
coveted—*wished for too much*

Jim had not yet seen his beautiful present. She held it out to him eagerly upon her open palm. The dull precious metal seemed to flash with a reflection of her bright and ardent spirit.

"Isn't it a dandy, Jim? I hunted all over town to find it. You'll have to look at the time a hundred times a day now. Give me your watch. I want to see how it looks on it."

Instead of obeying, Jim tumbled down on the couch and put his hands under the back of his head and smiled.

"Dell," said he, "let's put our Christmas presents away and keep 'em awhile. They're too nice to use just at present. I sold the watch to get the money to buy your combs. And now suppose you put the chops on."

The magi, as you know, were wise men—wonderfully wise men—who brought gifts to the Babe in the manger. They invented the art of giving Christmas presents. Being wise, their gifts were no doubt wise ones, possibly bearing the privilege of exchange in case of duplication. And here I have lamely not too well related to you the uneventful chronicle of two foolish children in a flat who most unwisely sacrificed for each other the greatest treasures of their house. But in a last word to the wise of these days let it be said that of all who give gifts these two were the wisest. Of all who give and receive gifts, such as they are wisest. Everywhere they are wisest. They are the magi.

ardent—*warm, passionate*

MAMMON AND THE ARCHER

1906

Mammon" means wealth: it is the name given in the New Testament (Matthew 6.24) to a personification, or mythical figure representing some general idea, of riches. "The Archer" here refers to Cupid, the Roman god of love. When people are hit by his golden arrows, they fall in love, and when hit by his leaden ones, they fall out of it. This is a story of Love and Money among the very rich. As is so often the case with O. Henry, a popular sentimental view of things—in this case, the one held by Richard's Aunt Ellen about Wealth and True Love—is tested by what happens in the action. The generally comical nature of "Mammon and the Archer" is made clear right at the beginning, in the contrast between the clever, practical man who has made his own fortune and his more snobbish neighbors on Fifth Avenue, who have inherited theirs. The comic name "G. Van Skuylight Suffolk-Jones" mocks both the oldest Dutch and the almost-as-old British aristocratic New York family names. That of Mr. Rockwall suggests strength and toughness along with what we see to be his good humor and lack of reverence even for the money he has made (he calls it "the great god Mazuma"). These are the qualities which allow him to take such effective steps to bring about a standard sort of happy ending to a tale of New York rather different from the others collected here.

Old Anthony Rockwall, retired manufacturer and proprietor of Rockwall's Eureka Soap, looked out the library window of his Fifth Avenue mansion and grinned. His neighbor to the right—the aristocratic clubman, G. Van Schuylight Suffolk-Jones—came out to his waiting motor-car, wrinkling a contumelious nostril, as usual, at the Italian renaissance sculpture of the soap palace's front elevation.

"Stuck-up old statuette of nothing doing!" commented the ex-Soap King. "The Eden Musee'll get that old frozen Nesselrode yet if he don't watch out. I'll have this house painted red, white, and blue next summer and see if that'll make his Dutch nose turn up any higher."

And then Anthony Rockwall, who never cared for bells, went to the door of his library and shouted "Mike!" in the same voice that had once chipped off pieces of the welkin on the Kansas prairies.

"Tell my son," said Anthony to the answering menial, "to come in here before he leaves the house."

When young Rockwall entered the library the old

clubman—*rich person active in the life of one or more city clubs*
contumelious—*contemptuous, insolent*
front elevation—*front view of a building*
Eden Musee'll—*theater and wax-works museum*
Nesselrode—*pudding or pie made with chestnuts and dried fruit*
welkin—*sky*
menial—*servant*

man laid aside his newspaper, looked at him with a kindly grimness on his big, smooth, ruddy countenance, rumpled his mop of white hair with one hand and rattled the keys in his pocket with the other.

"Richard," said Anthony Rockwall, "what do you pay for the soap that you use?"

Richard, only six months home from college, was startled a little.

He had not yet taken the measure of this sire of his, who was as full of unexpectednesses as a girl at her first party.

"Six dollars a dozen, I think, dad."

"And your clothes?"

"I suppose about sixty dollars, as a rule."

"You're a gentleman," said Anthony, decidedly. "I've heard of these young bloods spending twenty-four dollars a dozen for soap, and going over the hundred mark for clothes. You've got as much money to waste as any of 'em, and yet you stick to what's decent and moderate. Now I use the old Eureka—not only for sentiment, but it's the purest soap made. Whenever you pay more than ten cents a cake for soap you buy bad perfumes and labels. But fifty cents is doing very well for a young man in your generation, position and condition. As I said, you're a gentleman. They say it takes three generations to make one. They're off. Money'll do it as slick as soap grease. It's made you one. By hokey! It's almost made one of me. I'm nearly as impolite and disagreeable and ill-mannered as these two old Knickerbocker gents on each side of me that can't sleep of nights because I bought in between 'em."

"There are some things that money can't accomplish," remarked young Rockwall, rather gloomily.

"Now, don't say that," said old Anthony, shocked. "I bet my money on money every time. I've been through the encyclopaedia down to Y looking for something you can't buy with it; and I expect to have to take up the appendix

ruddy countenance—*healthy, reddish complexion*
Knickerbocker gents—*New Yorkers*
appendix—*additional material at the end of a book*

next week. I'm for money against the field. Tell me something money won't buy."

"For one thing," answered Richard, rankling a little, "it won't buy one into the exclusive circles of society."

"Oho! won't it?" thundered the champion of the root of evil. "You tell me where your exclusive circles would be if the first Astor hadn't had the money to pay for his steerage passage over?"

Richard sighed.

"And that's what I was coming to," said the old man, less boisterously. "That's why I asked you to come in. There's something going wrong with you, boy. I've been noticing it for two weeks. Out with it. I guess I could lay my hands on eleven millions within twenty-four hours, besides the real estate. If it's your liver, there's the Rambler down in the bay, coaled, and ready to steam down to the Bahamas in two days."

"Not a bad guess, dad; you haven't missed it far."

"Ah," said Anthony, keenly; "what's her name?"

Richard began to walk up and down the library floor. There was enough comradeship and sympathy in this crude old father of his to draw his confidence.

"Why don't you ask her?" demanded old Anthony. "She'll jump at you. You've got the money and the looks, and you're a decent boy. Your hands are clean. You've got no Eureka soap on 'em. You've been to college, but she'll overlook that."

"I haven't had a chance," said Richard.

the root of evil—*money, in an old proverb*
Astor—*the Astors were spoken of as the most aristocratic New York family*
steerage—*cheapest fare on steamships*
boisterously—*noisily*
the Rambler—*his yacht*
Bahamas—*islands in the Caribbean which were a playground of the very rich*

"Make one," said Anthony. "Take her for a walk in the park, or a straw ride, or walk home with her from church. Chance! Pshaw!"

"You don't know the social mill, dad. She's part of the stream that turns it. Every hour and minute of her time is arranged for days in advance. I must have that girl, dad, or this town is a blackjack swamp forevermore. And I can't write it—I can't do that."

"Tut!" said the old man. "Do you mean to tell me that with all the money I've got you can't get an hour or two of a girl's time for yourself?"

"I've put it off too late. She's going to sail for Europe at noon day after tomorrow for a two years' stay. I'm to see her alone tomorrow evening for a few minutes. She's at Larchmont now at her aunt's. I can't go there. But I'm allowed to meet her with a cab at the Grand Central Station tomorrow evening at the 8:30 train. We drive down Broadway to Wallack's at a gallop, where her mother and a box party will be waiting for us in the lobby. Do you think she would listen to a declaration from me during that six or eight minutes under those circumstances? No. And what chance would I have in the theatre or afterward? None. No, dad, this is one tangle that your money can't unravel. We can't buy one minute of time with cash; if we could, rich people would live longer. There's no hope of getting a talk with Miss Lantry before she sails."

"All right, Richard, my boy," said old Anthony, cheerfully. "You may run along down to your club now. I'm glad it ain't your liver. But don't forget to burn a few punk sticks in the joss house to the great god Mazuma from time to time. You say money won't buy time? Well, of course, you can't order eternity wrapped up and delivered at your residence for a price, but I've seen Father

Pshaw!—*"No way!"*
blackjack swamp—*entangling growth of shrub-like blackjack oaks*
Larchmont—*wealthy suburb of New York City*
Wallack's—*famous theater in Manhattan, then at Broadway and 30th Street*
your liver—*your liver which will suffer from over-eating and drinking*
punk sticks—*sticks of incense*
joss house—*Hindu temple*
Mazuma—*joking slang for "money"*

Time get pretty bad stone bruises on his heels when he walked through the gold diggings."

That night came Aunt Ellen, gentle, sentimental, wrinkled, sighing, oppressed by wealth, in to Brother Anthony at his evening paper, and began discourse on the subject of lovers' woes.

"He told me all about it," said brother Anthony, yawning. "I told him my bank account was at his service. And then he began to knock money. Said money couldn't help. Said the rules of society couldn't be bucked for a yard by a team of ten millionaires."

"Oh, Anthony," sighed Aunt Ellen, "I wish you would not think so much of money. Wealth is nothing where a true affection is concerned. Love is all-powerful. If he only had spoken earlier! She could not have refused our Richard. But now I fear it is too late. He will have no opportunity to address her. All your gold cannot bring happiness to your son."

At eight o'clock the next evening Aunt Ellen took a quaint old gold ring from a moth-eaten case and gave it to Richard.

"Wear it to-night, nephew," she begged. "Your mother gave it to me. Good luck in love she said it brought. She asked me to give it to you when you had found the one you loved."

Young Rockwall took the ring reverently and tried it on his smallest finger. It slipped as far as the second joint and stopped. He took it off and stuffed it into his vest pocket, after the manner of man. And then he 'phoned for his cab.

At the station he captured Miss Lantry out of the gadding mob at eight thirty-two.

"We mustn't keep mamma and the others waiting," said she.

"To Wallack's Theatre as fast as you can drive!" said Richard loyally.

They whirled up Forty-second to Broadway, and then down the white-starred lane that leads from the soft meadows of sunset to the rocky hills of morning.

At Thirty-fourth Street young Richard quickly thrust up the trap and ordered the cabman to stop.

"I've dropped a ring," he apologised, as he climbed out. "It was my mother's, and I'd hate to lose it. I won't detain you a minute—I saw where it fell."

In less than a minute he was back in the cab with the ring.

But within that minute a crosstown car had stopped directly in front of the cab. The cabman tried to pass to the left, but a heavy express wagon cut him off. He tried the right, and had to back away from a furniture van that had

after the manner of man—*as men will do*
gadding mob—*roaming about or rambling crowd*
express—*delivery*

KNICKER

no business to be there. He tried to back out, but dropped his reins and swore dutifully. He was blockaded in a tangled mess of vehicles and horses.

One of those street blockades had occurred that sometimes tie up commerce and movement quite suddenly in the big city.

"Why don't you drive on?" said Miss Lantry, impatiently. "We'll be late."

Richard stood up in the cab and looked around. He saw a congested flood of wagons, trucks, cabs, vans and street cars filling the vast space where Broadway, Sixth Avenue and Thirty-fourth Street cross one another as a twenty-six inch maiden fills her twenty-two inch girdle. And still from all the cross streets they were hurrying and rattling toward the converging point at full speed, and hurling themselves into the struggling mass, locking wheels and adding their drivers' imprecations to the clamor. The entire traffic of Manhattan seemed to have jammed itself around them. The oldest New Yorker among the thousands of spectators that lined the sidewalks had not witnessed a street blockade of the proportions of this one.

"I'm very sorry," said Richard, as he resumed his seat, "but it looks as if we are stuck. They won't get this jumble loosened up in an hour. It was my fault. If I hadn't dropped the ring we—"Let me see the ring," said Miss Lantry. "Now that it can't be helped, I don't care. I think theatres are stupid, anyway."

blockades—*traffic jams*
imprecations—*curses*

At eleven o'clock that night somebody tapped lightly on Anthony Rockwall's door.

"Come in," shouted Anthony, who was in a red dressing-gown, reading a book of piratical adventures.

Somebody was Aunt Ellen, looking like a grey-haired angel that had been left on earth by mistake.

"They're engaged, Anthony," she said, softly. "She has promised to marry our Richard. On their way to the theatre there was a street blockade, and it was two hours before their cab could get out of it.

"And oh, brother Anthony, don't ever boast of the power of money again. A little emblem of true love—a little ring that symbolized unending and unmercenary affection—was the cause of our Richard finding his happiness. He dropped it in the street, and got out to recover it. And before they could continue the blockade occurred. He spoke to his love and won her there while the cab was hemmed in. Money is dross compared with true love, Anthony."

"All right," said old Anthony. "I'm glad the boy has got what he wanted. I told him I wouldn't spare any expense in the matter if—"

"But, brother Anthony, what good could your money have done?"

"Sister," said Anthony Rockwall. "I've got my pirate in a devil of a scrape. His ship has just been scuttled, and he's too good a judge of the value of money to let drown. I wish you would let me go on with this chapter."

The story should end here. I wish it would as heartily as you who read it wish it did. But we must go to the bottom of the well for truth.

The next day a person with red hands and a blue polka-dot necktie, who called himself Kelly, called at Anthony Rockwall's house, and was at once received in the library.

"Well," said Anthony, reaching for his chequebook, "it was a good bilin' of soap. Let's see—you had five thousand dollars in cash."

"I paid out three hundred dollars more of my own," said Kelly. "I had to

piratical adventures—*pirate adventure stories*
unmercenary—*having nothing to do with money*
dross—*worthless stuff*
scuttled—*sunk by drilling holes in its hull*
the bottom of the well for truth—*referring to the old proverb, "The truth lies at the bottom of a well"*
bilin' of—*a lot of*

go a little above the estimate. I got the express wagons and cabs mostly for five dollars; but the trucks and two-horse teams mostly raised me to ten dollars. The motormen wanted ten dollars, and some of the loaded teams twenty dollars. The cops struck me hardest—fifty dollars I paid two, and the rest twenty and twenty-five dollars. But didn't it work beautiful, Mr. Rockwall? I'm glad William A. Brady wasn't onto that little outdoor vehicle mob scene. I wouldn't want William to break his heart with jealousy. And never a rehearsal, either! The boys was on time to the fraction of a second. It was two hours before a snake could get below Greeley's statue."

"Thirteen hundred—there you are, Kelly," said Anthony, tearing off a check. "Your thousand, and the three hundred you were out. You don't despise money, do you, Kelly?"

"Me?" said Kelly. "I can lick the man that invented poverty."

Anthony called Kelly when he was at the door.

"You didn't notice," said he, "anywhere in the tie-up, a kind of a fat boy without any clothes on shooting arrows around with a bow, did you?"

"Why, no," said Kelly, mystified. "I didn't. If he was like you say, maybe the cops pinched him before I got there."

"I thought the little rascal wouldn't be on hand," chuckled Anthony. "Good-by, Kelly."

William A. Brady—*famous boxing manager and, later, theatrical producer*

Greeley's statue—*statue of Horace Greeley, famous newspaper editor, at the crossing of Broadway and Sixth Avenue*

fat boy without any clothes on shooting arrows around with a bow—*Cupid, the Roman god of Love*

pinched—*arrested*

AFTER TWENTY YEARS

1906

This is the story of two friends separated for a long time who meet again as they had promised to do when they parted. Both of their lives have changed, and the New York City they both lived in has changed somewhat as well. They both keep their word, but their meeting takes an unexpected form. Bob, "the man from the West" in the story, whose self-regard has been "enlarged by success," doesn't notice something about the policeman that he should have. On the other hand, the same good qualities of character that honor both his duty to his job and consideration for a friend from the past lead Jimmy Wells to do what he does and to write the revealing letter at the end of the story. But did Jimmy keep the promised appointment out of the same loyalty to that early friendship that caused Bob to come from far away that night? Or was it only for another reason, which we learn of at the end? As they often must with the most interesting stories, readers will have to decide this for themselves.

THE POLICEMAN ON THE BEAT MOVED UP THE avenue impressively. The impressiveness was habitual and not for show, for spectators were few. The time was barely ten o'clock at night, but chilly gusts of wind with a taste of rain in them had well nigh depeopled the streets.

Trying doors as he went, twirling his club with many intricate and artful movements, turning now and then to cast his watchful eye adown the pacific thoroughfare, the officer, with his stalwart form and slight swagger, made a fine picture of a guardian of the peace. The vicinity was one that kept early hours. Now and then you might see the lights of a cigar store or of an all-night lunch counter; but the majority of the doors belonged to business places that had long since been closed.

When about midway of a certain block the policeman suddenly slowed his walk. In the doorway of a darkened hardware store a man leaned, with an unlighted cigar in his mouth. As the policeman walked up to him the man spoke up quickly.

"It's all right, officer," he said, reassuringly. "I'm just waiting for a friend. It's an appointment made twenty years ago. Sounds a little funny to you, doesn't it? Well, I'll explain if you'd like to make certain it's all straight. About that long ago there used to be a restaurant where this store stands—'Big Joe' Brady's restaurant."

"Until five years ago," said the policeman. "It was torn down then."

The man in the doorway struck a match and lit his cigar. The light showed a pale, square-jawed face with keen eyes, and a little white scar near his right eyebrow. His scarfpin was a large diamond, oddly set.

"Twenty years ago to-night," said the man, "I dined here at 'Big Joe' Brady's with Jimmy Wells, my best chum, and the finest chap in the world. He and I were raised here in New York, just like two brothers, together. I was eighteen and Jimmy was twenty. The next morning I was to start for the West to make my fortune. You couldn't have dragged Jimmy out of New York; he thought it was the only place on earth. Well, we agreed that night that

depeopled—*emptied of people*
stalwart—*strong, sturdy*
swagger—*boastful way of walking*
chum—*friend*

we would meet here again exactly twenty years from that date and time, no matter what our conditions might be or from what distance we might have to come. We figured that in twenty years each of us ought to have our destiny worked out and our fortunes made, whatever they were going to be."

"It sounds pretty interesting," said the policeman. "Rather a long time between meets, though, it seems to me. Haven't you heard from your friend since you left?"

"Well, yes, for a time we corresponded," said the other. "But after a year or two we lost track of each other. You see, the West is a pretty big proposition, and I kept hustling around over it pretty lively. But I know Jimmy will meet me here if he's alive, for he always was the truest, stanchest old chap in the world. He'll never forget. I came a thousand miles to stand in this door to-night, and it's worth it if my old partner turns up."

The waiting man pulled out a handsome watch, the lids of it set with small diamonds.

"Three minutes to ten," he announced. "It was exactly ten o'clock when we parted here at the restaurant door."

"Did pretty well out West, didn't you?" asked the policeman.

"You bet! I hope Jimmy has done half as well. He was a kind of plodder, though, good fellow as he was. I've had to compete with some of the sharpest wits going to get my pile. A man gets in a groove in New York. It takes the West to put a razor-edge on him."

The policeman twirled his club and took a step or two.

stanchest—*most faithful*
plodder—*someone who moves heavily and slowly*
gets in a groove—*gets stuck in a rut, doing the same thing all the time*

"I'll be on my way. Hope your friend comes around all right. Going to call time on him sharp?"

"I should say not!" said the other. "I'll give him half an hour at least. If Jimmy is alive on earth he'll be here by that time. So long, officer."

"Good-night, sir," said the policeman, passing on along his beat, trying doors as he went.

There was now a fine, cold drizzle falling, and the wind had risen from its uncertain puffs into a steady blow. The few foot passengers astir in that quarter hurried dismally and silently along with coat collars turned high and pocketed hands. And in the door of the hardware store the man who had come a thousand miles to fill an appointment, uncertain almost to absurdity, with the friend of his youth, smoked his cigar and waited.

About twenty minutes he waited, and then a tall man in a long overcoat, with collar turned up to his ears, hurried across from the opposite side of the street. He went directly to the waiting man.

"Is that you, Bob?" he asked, doubtfully.

"Is that you, Jimmy Wells?" cried the man in the door.

"Bless my heart!" exclaimed the new arrival, grasping both the other's hands with his own. "It's Bob, sure as fate. I was certain I'd find you here if you were still in existence. Well, well, well!—twenty years is a long time. The old restaurant's gone, Bob; I wish it had lasted, so we could have had another dinner there. How has the West treated you, old man?"

"Bully; it has given me everything I asked it for. You've changed lots, Jimmy. I never thought you were so tall by two or three inches."

"Oh, I grew a bit after I was twenty."

"Doing well in New York, Jimmy?"

"Moderately. I have a position in one of the city departments. Come on, Bob; we'll go around to a place I know of, and have a good long talk about old times."

The two men started up the street, arm in arm. The man from the West, his egotism enlarged by success, was beginning to outline the history of

uncertain almost to absurdity—*completely unsure of meeting him*

his career. The other, submerged in his overcoat, listened with interest.

At the corner stood a drug store, brilliant with electric lights.

When they came into this glare each of them turned simultaneously to gaze upon the other's face.

The man from the West stopped suddenly and released his arm.

"You're not Jimmy Wells," he snapped. "Twenty years is a long time, but not long enough to change a man's nose from a Roman to a pug."

"It sometimes changes a good man into a bad one," said the tall man.

"You've been under arrest for ten minutes, 'Silky' Bob. Chicago thinks you may have dropped over our way and wires us she wants to have a chat with you. Going quietly, are you? That's sensible. Now, before we go on to the station here's a note I was asked to hand you. You may read it here at the window. It's from Patrolman Wells."

The man from the West unfolded the little piece of paper handed him. His hand was steady when he began to read, but it trembled a little by the time he had finished. The note was rather short.

"Bob: I was at the appointed place on time. When you struck the match to light your cigar I saw it was the face of the man wanted in Chicago. Somehow I couldn't do it myself, so I went around and got a plain clothes man to do the job. JIMMY."

egotism—*sense of his own importance*
simultaneously—*at the same time*
Roman—*with a high bridge*
pug—*somewhat flat with a turned-up end*
Chicago—*the Chicago police*

TWO THANKSGIVING DAY GENTLEMEN

1907

This story can be read as a companion piece to "The Gift of the Magi." A Thanksgiving rather than Christmas story, it also concerns the meaning of giving and receiving. It has its ironies too, but they are sadder and more harsh. The Old Gentleman has been treating the "bum" (as some unemployed men were called then) Stuffy Pete to Thanksgiving dinner for nine years, and we learn that doing so has become an important annual event for him. The plot turns on Stuffy's understanding and practice of charity and his comic attempt to befriend the Old Gentleman. Only at the end do we discover hidden aspects of their two conditions of life that may change what we think about charity and customs.

The story takes place at Union Square in Manhattan, between Broadway and Fourth Avenue on Fourteenth Street. Here again we should remember the value of money at the time. The huge meal—at a good but not grand restaurant—costs a dollar thirty and the Old Gentleman leaves a fifteen cent tip (about twelve percent). But in another O. Henry story, "An Unfinished Story," a very poor shop girl named Dulcie, who earns four dollars a week, treats herself on Sundays to veal chops and pineapple fritters for twenty-five cents, and leaves a forty percent tip of a dime. Consider who tips at a higher rate, and think why. Does this add to the irony of the ending?

THERE IS ONE DAY THAT IS OURS. THERE IS ONE day when all we Americans who are not self-made go back to the old home to eat saleratus biscuits and marvel how much nearer to the porch the old pump looks than it used to. Bless the day. President Roosevelt gives it to us. We hear some talk of the Puritans, but don't just remember who they were. Bet we can lick 'em, anyhow, if they try to land again. Plymouth Rocks? Well, that sounds more familiar. Lots of us have had to come down to hens since the Turkey Trust got its work in. But somebody in Washington is leaking out advance information to 'em about these Thanksgiving proclamations. The big city east of the cranberry bogs has made Thanksgiving Day an institution. The last Thursday in November is the only day in the year on which it recognizes the part of America lying across the ferries. It is the one day that is purely American. Yes, a day of celebration, exclusively American.

And now for the story which is to prove to you that we have traditions on this side of the ocean that are becoming older at a much rapider rate than those of England are thanks to our git-up and enterprise.

Stuffy Pete took his seat on the third bench to the right as you enter Union Square from the east, at the walk opposite the fountain.

Every Thanksgiving Day for nine years he had taken his seat there promptly at one o'clock. For every time he had done so things had happened to him Charles Dickensy things that swelled his waistcoat above his heart, and equally on the other side.

But to-day Stuffy Pete's appearance at the annual trysting place seemed to have been rather the result of habit than of the yearly hunger which, as the philanthropists seem to think, afflicts the poor at such extended intervals.

saleratus—*soda*
President Roosevelt gives it to us—*Theodore Roosevelt made Thanksgiving Day an official holiday*
Turkey Trust—*as if the establishing of Thanksgiving were a scheme of a turkey industry to sell more turkeys—a joke in those days*
git-up—*"get-up-and-go," an older slang term for energy in work or business*
Charles Dickensy—*charitable gifts of food, like those in some novels of Dickens*
trysting—*meeting*

Certainly Pete was not hungry. He had just come from a feast that had left him of his powers barely those of respiration and locomotion. His eyes were like two pale gooseberries firmly imbedded in a swollen and gravy-smeared mask of putty. His breath came in short wheezes; a senatorial roll of adipose tissue denied a fashionable set to his upturned coat collar. Buttons that had been sewed upon his clothes by kind Salvation fingers a week before flew like popcorn; strewing the earth around him. Ragged he was, with a split shirt front open to the wishbone; but the November breeze, carrying fine snowflakes, brought him only a grateful coolness. For Stuffy Pete was overcharged with the caloric produced by a superbountiful dinner, beginning with oysters and ending with plum pudding, and including (it seemed to him) all the roast turkey and baked potatoes and chicken salad and squash pie and ice cream in the world. Wherefore he sat, gorged, and gazed upon the world with after-dinner contempt.

The meal had been an unexpected one. He was passing a red brick mansion near the beginning of Fifth avenue, in which lived two old ladies of ancient family and a reverence for traditions. They even denied the existence of New York, and believed that Thanksgiving Day was declared solely for Washington Square. One of their traditional habits was to station a servant at the postern gate with orders to admit the first hungry wayfarer that came along after the hour of noon had struck, and banquet him to a finish. Stuffy Pete happened to

respiration—*breathing*
adipose—*fat*
Salvation—*Salvation Army*
caloric—*number of calories*
gorged—*stuffed himself*
postern—*rear*

pass by on his way to the park, and the seneschals gathered him in and upheld the custom of the castle.

After Stuffy Pete had gazed straight before him for ten minutes he was conscious of a desire for a more varied field of vision. With a tremendous effort he moved his head slowly to the left. And then his eyes bulged out fearfully, and his breath ceased, and the rough-shod ends of his short legs wriggled and rustled on the gravel.

For the Old Gentleman was coming across Fourth avenue toward his bench.

Every Thanksgiving Day for nine years the Old Gentleman had come there and found Stuffy Pete on his bench. That was a thing that the Old Gentleman was trying to make a tradition of. Every Thanksgiving Day for nine years he had found Stuffy there, and had led him to a restaurant and watched him eat a big dinner. They do those things in England unconsciously. But this is a young country, and nine years is not so bad. The Old Gentleman was a staunch American patriot, and considered himself a pioneer in American tradition. In order to become picturesque we must keep on doing one thing for a long time without ever letting it get away from us. Something like collecting the weekly dimes in industrial insurance. Or cleaning the streets.

The Old Gentleman moved, straight and stately, toward the Institution that he was rearing. Truly, the annual feeding of Stuffy Pete was nothing national in its character, such as the Magna Charta or jam for breakfast was in England. But it was a step. It was almost feudal. It showed, at least, that a Custom was not impossible to New Y—ahem!—America.

The Old Gentleman was thin and tall and sixty. He was dressed all in black, and wore the old-fashioned kind of glasses that won't stay on your nose. His

seneschals—*stewards in a castle*
rough-shod—*in very worn shoes*
Magna Charta—*the great agreement of King John in 1215 guaranteeing political liberties to the English nobility*
feudal—*how people were ranked in society in he Middle Ages*

hair was whiter and thinner than it had been last year, and he seemed to make more use of his big, knobby cane with the crooked handle.

As his established benefactor came up Stuffy wheezed and shuddered like some woman's over-fat pug when a street dog bristles up at him.

He would have flown, but all the skill of Santos-Dumont could not have separated him from his bench. Well had the myrmidons of the two old ladies done their work.

"Good morning," said the Old Gentleman. "I am glad to perceive that the vicissitudes of another year have spared you to move in health about the beautiful world. For that blessing alone this day of thanksgiving is well proclaimed to each of us. If you will come with me, my man, I will provide you with a dinner that should make your physical being accord with the mental."

That is what the old Gentleman said every time. Every Thanksgiving Day for nine years. The words themselves almost formed an Institution. Nothing could be compared with them except the Declaration of Independence. Always before they had been music in Stuffy's ears. But now he looked up at the Old Gentleman's face with tearful agony in his own. The fine snow almost sizzled when it fell upon his perspiring brow. But the Old Gentleman shivered a little and turned his back to the wind.

Stuffy had always wondered why the Old Gentleman spoke his speech rather sadly. He did not know that it was because he was wishing every time that he had a son to succeed him. A son who would come there after he was

Santos-Dumont—*famous aviator—he flew a powered airship two years before the Wright brothers*
myrmidons—*blindly loyal servants*
vicissitudes—*changes in luck*

gone—a son who would stand proud and strong before some subsequent Stuffy, and say: "In memory of my father."

Then it would be an Institution.

But the Old Gentleman had no relatives. He lived in rented rooms in one of the decayed old family brownstone mansions in one of the quiet streets east of the park. In the winter he raised fuchsias in a little conservatory the size of a steamer trunk. In the spring he walked in the Easter parade. In the summer he lived at a farmhouse in the New Jersey hills, and sat in a wicker armchair, speaking of a butterfly, the *ornithoptera amphrisius*, that he hoped to find some day. In the autumn he fed Stuffy a dinner. These were the Old Gentleman's occupations.

Stuffy Pete looked up at him for a half minute, stewing and helpless in his own self-pity. The Old Gentleman's eyes were bright with the giving-pleasure. His face was getting more lined each year, but his little black necktie was in as jaunty a bow as ever, and the linen was beautiful and white, and his gray mustache was curled carefully at the ends. And then Stuffy made a noise that sounded like peas bubbling in a pot. Speech was intended; and as the Old Gentleman had heard the sounds nine times before, he rightly construed them into Stuffy's old formula of acceptance.

"Thankee, sir. I'll go with ye, and much obliged. I'm very hungry, sir."

The coma of repletion had not prevented from entering Stuffy's mind the conviction that he was the basis of an Institution. His Thanksgiving appetite was not his own; it belonged by all the sacred rights of established custom, if not, by the actual Statute of Limitations, to this kind old gentleman who had preempted it. True, America is free; but in order to establish tradition someone must be a

steamer trunk—*large trunk for use in cabins of steamships, which, when stood on end and opened, had room for drawers on one side, and hanging clothes on the other*
construed them into—*understood them as*
coma of repletion—*being groggy from having eaten too much*
Statute of Limitations—*the law that prevents anyone from being prosecuted for any crime except murder, after seven years*
preempted it—*claimed it by right*

repetend—a repeating decimal. The heroes are not all heroes of steel and gold. See one here that wielded only weapons of iron, badly silvered, and tin.

The Old Gentleman led his annual protégé southward to the restaurant, and to the table where the feast had always occurred.

They were recognized.

"Here comes de old guy," said a waiter, "dat blows dat same bum to a meal every Thanksgiving."

The Old Gentleman sat across the table glowing like a smoked pearl at his cornerstone of future ancient Tradition. The waiters heaped the table with holiday food—and Stuffy, with a sigh that was mistaken for hunger's expression, raised knife and fork and carved for himself a crown of imperishable bay No more valiant hero ever fought his way through the ranks of an enemy. Turkey, chops, soups, vegetables, pies, disappeared before him as fast as they could be served. Gorged nearly to the uttermost when he entered the restaurant, the smell of food had almost caused him to lose his honor as a gentleman, but he rallied like a true knight. He saw the look of beneficent happiness on the Old Gentleman's face—a happier look than even the fuchsias and the *ornithoptera amphrisiushad* ever brought to it—and he had not the heart to see it wane.

In an hour Stuffy leaned back with a battle won. "Thankee kindly, sir," he puffed like a leaky steam pipe; "thankee kindly for a hearty meal." Then he arose heavily with glazed eyes and started toward the kitchen. A waiter turned him about like a top, and pointed him toward the door. The Old Gentleman

smoked pearl—*pearl given a deeper glow*
a crown of imperishable bay—*undying (because evergreen) laurel: in ancient Rome, the crown given to great leaders in battle*
wane—*fade, lessen*

carefully counted out a dollar, thirty in silver change, leaving three nickels for the waiter.

They parted as they did each year at the door, the Old Gentleman going south, Stuffy north.

Around the first corner Stuffy turned, and stood for one minute.

Then he seemed to puff out his rags as an owl puffs out his feathers, and fell to the sidewalk like a sun-stricken horse.

When the ambulance came the young surgeon and the driver cursed softly at his weight. There was no smell of whiskey to justify a transfer to the patrol wagon, so Stuffy and his two dinners went to the hospital. There they stretched him on a bed and began to test him for strange diseases, with the hope of getting a chance at some problem with the bare steel.

And lo! an hour later another ambulance brought the Old Gentleman.

And they laid him on another bed and spoke of appendicitis, for he looked good for the bill.

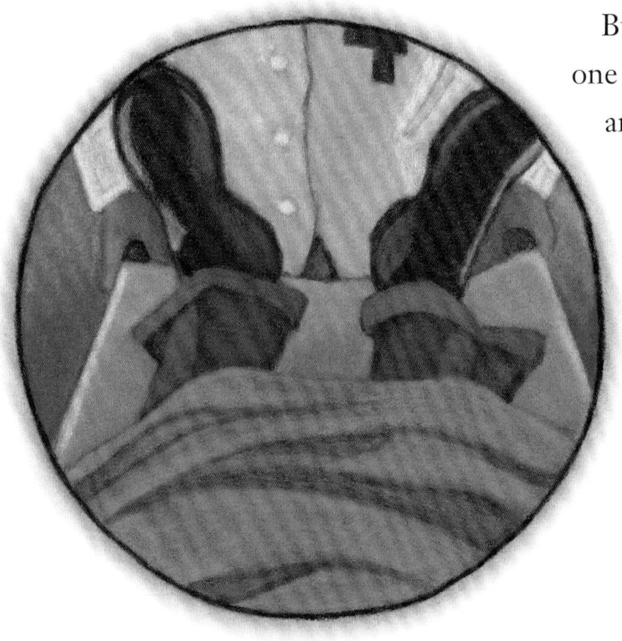

But pretty soon one of the young doctors met one of the young nurses whose eyes he liked, and stopped to chat with her about the cases.

"That nice old gentleman over there, now," he said, "you wouldn't think that was a case of almost starvation. Proud old family, I guess. He told me he hadn't eaten a thing for three days."

bare steel—*a chance to operate on him*

THE LAST LEAF

1907

Greenwich Village is a region of lower Manhattan, just south and west of Union Square. At the beginning of the twentieth century, it had recently become a place where artists and writers, many from all over the United States, lived and had their studios. "The Last Leaf" tells of an artist like those in Puccini's famous opera La Bohème*—in fact, O. Henry had been reading, in the French book from which the opera's story was drawn, of a poor hatmaker in Paris who waters the shop's flowers at night to keep them alive. He had also recently been shown by a friend a rear tenement at the corner of Grove and Hudson streets, where he seems to imagine the story taking place. "The lifetime of the flowers," he wrote later, "was to be the lifetime of that transient love." But in "The Last Leaf," written shortly thereafter, the matter is more complex and interesting. It involves not flowers, but leaves. A leaf on a tree as a symbol for a human life is as old as the very beginnings of our literature; and here the lifetime of an actual leaf on an ivy vine and that of two different people are strangely and surprisingly connected. That the people involved —Johnsy and old Mr. Behrman—are artists is essential to the outcome. The reader will find two surprises at the ending, one after another. In the first of these, we see how Johnsy had been wrong about a leaf and a life; in the second, just after that one, it appears that she had been right, in one way, after all.*

IN A LITTLE DISTRICT WEST OF WASHINGTON Square the streets have run crazy and broken themselves into small strips called "places." These "places" make strange angles and curves. One street crosses itself a time or two. An artist once discovered a valuable possibility in this street. Suppose a collector with a bill for paints, paper and canvas should, in traversing this route, suddenly meet himself coming back, without a cent having been paid on account!

So, to quaint old Greenwich Village the art people soon came prowling, hunting for north windows and eighteenth-century gables and Dutch attics and low rents. Then they imported some pewter mugs and a chafing dish or two from Sixth Avenue, and became a "colony."

At the top of a squatty, three-story brick Sue and Johnsy had their studio. "Johnsy" was familiar for Joanna. One was from Maine; the other from California. They had met at the table d'hote of an Eighth Street "Delmonico's," and found their tastes in art, chicory salad and bishop sleeves so congenial that the joint studio resulted.

That was in May. In November a cold, unseen stranger, whom the doctors called Pneumonia, stalked about the colony, touching one here and there with his icy fingers. Over on the east side this ravager strode boldly, smiting his victims by scores, but his feet trod slowly through the maze of the narrow and moss-grown "places."

Suppose a collector—*this suggests the streets were so confusing no one could find you if you didn't want them to*
north windows—*because artists want north light in their studios*
gables—*triangular frames coming out over windows from a roof*
pewter—*a gray, heavy metal*
chafing dish—*metal dish with a small heater below it, to keep food warm at table*
table d'hote—*table at a restaurant where everyone sits together*
Delmonico's—*the real Delmonico's was a famous fancy restaurant in New York in those days*
bishop sleeves—*"bishop sleeves" on dresses and coats were full toward the top and gathered at the wrists, newly fashionable at the time*
ravager—*destroyer*

Mr. Pneumonia was not what you would call a chivalric old gentleman.

A mite of a little woman with blood thinned by California zephyrs was hardly fair game for the red-fisted, short-breathed old duffer.

But Johnsy he smote; and she lay, scarcely moving, on her painted iron bedstead, looking through the small Dutch window-panes at the blank side of the next brick house.

One morning the busy doctor invited Sue into the hallway with a shaggy, gray eyebrow.

"She has one chance in—let us say, ten," he said, as he shook down the mercury in his clinical thermometer. "And that chance is for her to want to live. This way people have of lining-up on the side of the undertaker makes the entire pharmacopeia look silly. Your little lady has made up her mind that she's not going to get well. Has she anything on her mind?"

"She—she wanted to paint the Bay of Naples some day," said Sue.

"Paint?—bosh! Has she anything on her mind worth thinking about twice—a man, for instance?"

"A man?" said Sue, with a Jew's harp twang in her voice. "Is a man worth—but, no, doctor; there is nothing of the kind."

"Well, it is the weakness, then," said the doctor. "I will do all that science, so far as it may filter through my efforts, can accomplish. But whenever my patient begins to count the carriages in her funeral procession I subtract fifty percent from the curative power of medicines. If you will get her to ask one

smote—*hit hard*
pharmacopeia—*official list of all medical drugs*
Jew's harp—*small metal instrument held in the mouth*

question about the new winter styles in cloak sleeves I will promise you a one-in-five chance for her, instead of one in ten."

After the doctor had gone Sue went into the workroom and cried a Japanese napkin to a pulp. Then she swaggered into Johnsy's room with her drawing board, whistling ragtime.

Johnsy lay, scarcely making a ripple under the bedclothes, with her face toward the window. Sue stopped whistling, thinking she was asleep.

She arranged her board and began a pen-and-ink drawing to illustrate a magazine story. Young artists must pave their way to Art by drawing pictures for magazine stories that young authors write to pave their way to Literature.

As Sue was sketching a pair of elegant horseshow riding trousers and a monocle on the figure of the hero, an Idaho cowboy, she heard a low sound, several times repeated. She went quickly to the bedside.

Johnsy's eyes were open wide. She was looking out the window and counting—counting backward.

"Twelve," she said, and a little later "eleven;" and then "ten," and "nine;" and then "eight" and "seven," almost together.

Sue looked solicitously out the window. What was there to count?

There was only a bare, dreary yard to be seen, and the blank side of the brick house twenty feet away. An old, old ivy vine, gnarled and decayed at the roots, climbed halfway up the brick wall. The cold breath of autumn had stricken its leaves from the vine until its skeleton branches clung, almost bare, to the crumbling bricks.

"What is it, dear?" asked Sue.

"Six," said Johnsy, in almost a whisper. "They're falling faster now. Three days ago there were almost a hundred. It made my head ache to count them. But now it's easy. There goes another one. There are only five left now."

"Five what, dear. Tell your Sudie."

"Leaves. On the ivy vine. When the last one falls I must go, too. I've known that for three days. Didn't the doctor tell you?"

Japanese napkin—*printed paper napkin, elaborately folded*

"Oh, I never heard of such nonsense," complained Sue, with magnificent scorn. "What have old ivy leaves to do with your getting well? And you used to love that vine so, you naughty girl. Don't be a goosey. Why, the doctor told me this morning that your chances for getting well real soon were—let's see exactly what he said—he said the chances were ten to one! Why, that's almost as good a chance as we have in New York when we ride on the street cars or walk past a new building. Try to take some broth now, and let Sudie go back to her drawing, so she can sell the editor man with it, and buy port wine for her sick child, and pork chops for her greedy self."

"You needn't get any more wine," said Johnsy, keeping her eyes fixed out the window. "There goes another. No, I don't want any broth.

That leaves just four. I want to see the last one fall before it gets dark. Then I'll go, too."

"Johnsy, dear," said Sue, bending over her, "will you promise me to keep your eyes closed, and not look out the window until I am done working? I must hand those drawings in by tomorrow. I need the light, or I would draw the shade down."

"Couldn't you draw in the other room?" asked Johnsy, coldly.

"I'd rather be here by you," said Sue. "Besides I don't want you to keep looking at those silly ivy leaves."

"Tell me as soon as you have finished," said Johnsy, closing her eyes, and lying white and still as a fallen statue, "because I want to see the last one fall. I'm tired of waiting. I'm tired of thinking. I want to turn loose my hold on everything, and go sailing down, down, just like one of those poor, tired leaves."

"Try to sleep," said Sue. "I must call Behrman up to be my model for the old hermit miner. I'll not be gone a minute. Don't try to move 'till I come back."

Old Behrman was a painter who lived on the ground floor beneath them. He was past sixty and had a Michael Angelo's Moses beard curling down from the head of a satyr along the body of an imp. Behrman was a failure in art. Forty years he had wielded the brush without getting near enough to touch the hem of his Mistress's robe. He had been always about to paint a masterpiece, but had never yet begun it. For several years he had painted nothing except now and then a daub in the line of commerce or advertising. He earned a little by serving as a model to those young artists in the colony who could not pay the price of a professional. He drank gin to excess, and still talked of his coming masterpiece. For the rest he was a fierce little old man, who scoffed terribly at softness in any one, and who regarded himself as especial mastiff-in-waiting to protect the two young artists in the studio above.

Sue found Behrman smelling strongly of juniper berries in his dimly lighted den below. In one corner was a blank canvas on an easel that had been waiting there for twenty-five years to receive the first line of the masterpiece. She told him of Johnsy's fancy, and how she feared she would, indeed, light and fragile as a leaf herself, float away when her slight hold upon the world grew weaker.

Old Behrman, with his red eyes, plainly streaming, shouted his contempt and derision for such idiotic imaginings.

"Vass!" he cried. "Is dere a people in de world mit der foolishness to die because leafs dey drop off from a confounded vine? I haf not heard of such a

Michael Angelo's Moses beard—*the long curly beard of Michelangelo's great seated sculpture of Moses*
satyr—*mythical half-goat, half-man*
imp—*a small demon or devil*
mastiff—*breed of huge dog*
derision—*scorn*
dere—*O. Henry imitates Mr. Behrman's German accent by having him use "d" for "th," and "b" for "p" and vice versa*
mit—*with*

thing. No, I will not bose as a model for your fool hermit-dunderhead. Vy do you allow dot silly pusiness to come in der prain of her? Ach, dot poor lettle Miss Johnsy."

"She is very ill and weak," said Sue, "and the fever has left her mind morbid and full of strange fancies. Very well, Mr. Behrman, if you do not care to pose for me, you needn't. But I think you are a horrid old—old flibbertigibbet."

"You are just like a woman!" yelled Behrman. "Who said I will not bose? Go on. I come mit you. For half an hour I haf peen trying to say dot I am ready to bose. Gott! dis is not any blace in which one so goot as Miss Yohnsy shall lie sick. Some day I vill baint a masterpiece, and ve shall all go away. Gott! yes."

Johnsy was sleeping when they went upstairs. Sue pulled the shade down to the window-sill, and motioned Behrman into the other room.

In there they peered out the window fearfully at the ivy vine. Then they looked at each other for a moment without speaking. A persistent, cold rain was falling, mingled with snow. Behrman, in his old blue shirt, took his seat as the hermit-miner on an upturned kettle for a rock.

When Sue awoke from an hour's sleep the next morning she found Johnsy with dull, wide-open eyes staring at the drawn green shade.

"Pull it up; I want to see," she ordered, in a whisper.

Wearily Sue obeyed.

But, lo! after the beating rain and fierce gusts of wind that had endured through the livelong night, there yet stood out against the brick wall one ivy leaf. It was the last on the vine. Still dark green near its stem, but with its serrated edges tinted with the yellow of dissolution and decay, it hung bravely from a branch some twenty feet above the ground.

"It is the last one," said Johnsy. "I thought it would surely fall during the night. I heard the wind. It will fall today, and I shall die at the same time."

"Dear, dear!" said Sue, leaning her worn face down to the pillow, "think of me, if you won't think of yourself. What would I do?"

But Johnsy did not answer. The lonesomest thing in all the world is a soul when it is making ready to go on its mysterious, far journey.

The fancy seemed to possess her more strongly as one by one the ties that bound her to friendship and to earth were loosed.

The day wore away, and even through the twilight they could see the lone ivy leaf clinging to its stem against the wall. And then, with the coming of the night the north wind was again loosed, while the rain still beat against the windows and pattered down from the low Dutch eaves.

When it was light enough Johnsy, the merciless, commanded that the shade be raised.

The ivy leaf was still there.

Johnsy lay for a long time looking at it. And then she called to Sue, who was stirring her chicken broth over the gas stove.

"I've been a bad girl, Sudie," said Johnsy. "Something has made that last leaf stay there to show me how wicked I was. It is a sin to want to die. You may bring me a little broth now, and some milk with a little port in it, and—no; bring me a hand-mirror first, and then pack some pillows about me, and I will sit up and watch you cook."

An hour later she said.

"Sudie, some day I hope to paint the Bay of Naples."

eaves—*lower edges of a roof*

The doctor came in the afternoon, and Sue had an excuse to go into the hallway as he left.

"Even chances," said the doctor, taking Sue's thin, shaking hand in his. "With good nursing you'll win. And now I must see another case I have downstairs. Behrman, his name is—some kind of an artist, I believe. Pneumonia, too. He is an old, weak man, and the attack is acute. There is no hope for him; but he goes to the hospital today to be made more comfortable."

The next day the doctor said to Sue: "She's out of danger. You've won. Nutrition and care now—that's all."

And that afternoon Sue came to the bed where Johnsy lay, contentedly knitting a very blue and very useless woolen shoulder scarf, and put one arm around her, pillows and all.

"I have something to tell you, white mouse," she said. "Mr. Behrman died of pneumonia today in the hospital. He was ill only two days.

The janitor found him on the morning of the first day in his room downstairs helpless with pain. His shoes and clothing were wet through and icy cold. They couldn't imagine where he had been on such a dreadful night. And then they found a lantern, still lighted, and a ladder that had been dragged from its place, and some scattered brushes, and a palette with green and yellow colors mixed on it, and—look out the window, dear, at the last ivy leaf on the wall. Didn't you wonder why it never fluttered or moved when the wind blew? Ah, darling, it's Behrman's masterpiece—he painted it there the night that the last leaf fell."

A RETRIEVED REFORMATION

1909

The reformation in this story is of a celebrated safecracker, just released from prison after having been pardoned as a result of illegal influence by friends. He is supposed to have "reformed," but his reformation disappears immediately, as soon as he can get back to his expensive and powerful tools again. But then he truly reforms because of his feeling for an attractive young woman. Ben Price, the detective, isn't fooled by the now-retired safecracker's new identity. He recognizes Ralph Spencer to be the criminal he has been pursuing, and assumes that his only interest in the Adams family is the vault in the father's bank. He does not recognize that Jimmy Valentine has indeed reformed, and is now living a virtuous and blameless life. On the other hand, when he sees what Jimmy is willing to do, out of love for his fiancée Annabel and concern for her niece, he acts in a surprising way. A particularly nice moment in this story occurs when Jimmy sets out on his rescue mission at the bank, the one he knows will result in his going to prison and losing his whole reformed life. He asks Annabel for a flower, and wears it as if he were a fairy-tale knight wearing his lady's glove or sleeve or handkerchief on his heroic mission.

A GUARD CAME TO THE PRISON SHOE SHOP, where Jimmy Valentine was assiduously stitching uppers, and escorted him to the front office. There the warden handed Jimmy his pardon, which had been signed that morning by the governor. Jimmy took it in a tired kind of way. He had served nearly ten months of a four year sentence. He had expected to stay only about three months, at the longest. When a man with as many friends on the outside as Jimmy Valentine had is received in the "stir" it is hardly worth while to cut his hair.

"Now, Valentine," said the warden, "you'll go out in the morning. Brace up, and make a man of yourself. You're not a bad fellow at heart. Stop cracking safes, and live straight."

"Me?" said Jimmy, in surprise. "Why, I never cracked a safe in my life."

"Oh, no," laughed the warden. "Of course not. Let's see, now. How was it you happened to get sent up on that Springfield job? Was it because you wouldn't prove an alibi for fear of compromising somebody in extremely high-toned society? Or was it simply a case of a mean old jury that had it in for you? It's always one or the other with you innocent victims."

assiduously—*attentively*
uppers—*upper parts of shoes*
"stir"—*jail*
cracking safes—*breaking into them*
alibi—*proof that one was elsewhere when a crime was committed*

"Me?" said Jimmy, still blankly virtuous. "Why, warden, I never was in Springfield in my life!"

"Take him back, Cronin!" said the warden, "and fix him up with outgoing clothes. Unlock him at seven in the morning, and let him come to the bull pen. Better think over my advice, Valentine."

At a quarter past seven on the next morning Jimmy stood in the warden's outer office. He had on a suit of the villainously fitting, ready-made clothes and a pair of the stiff, squeaky shoes that the state furnishes to its discharged compulsory guests.

The clerk handed him a railroad ticket and the five-dollar bill with which the law expected him to rehabilitate himself into good citizenship and prosperity. The warden gave him a cigar, and shook hands. Valentine, 9762, was chronicled on the books, "Pardoned by Governor," and Mr. James Valentine walked out into the sunshine.

Disregarding the song of the birds, the waving green trees, and the smell of the flowers, Jimmy headed straight for a restaurant. There he tasted the first sweet joys of liberty in the shape of a broiled chicken and a bottle of white wine—followed by a cigar a grade better than the one the warden had given him. From there he proceeded leisurely to the depot. He tossed a quarter into the hat of a blind man sitting by the door, and boarded his train. Three hours set him down in a little town near the state line. He went to the cafe of one Mike Dolan and shook hands with Mike, who was alone behind the bar.

"Sorry we couldn't make it sooner, Jimmy, me boy," said Mike. "But we had that protest from Springfield to buck against, and the governor nearly balked. Feeling all right?"

"Fine," said Jimmy. "Got my key?"

He got his key and went upstairs, unlocking the door of a room at the rear.

bull pen—*where prisoners are temporarily held*
villainously—*badly*
chronicled—*written*
balked—*changed his mind*

Everything was just as he had left it. There on the floor was still Ben Price's collar-button that had been torn from that eminent detective's shirt-band when they had overpowered Jimmy to arrest him.

Pulling out from the wall a folding bed, Jimmy slid back a panel in the wall and dragged out a dust-covered suitcase. He opened this and gazed fondly at the finest set of burglar's tools in the East. It was a complete set, made of specially tempered steel, the latest designs in drills, punches, braces and bits, jimmies, clamps, and augers, with two or three novelties, invented by Jimmy himself, in which he took pride. Over nine hundred dollars they had cost him to have made at——, a place where they make such things for the profession.

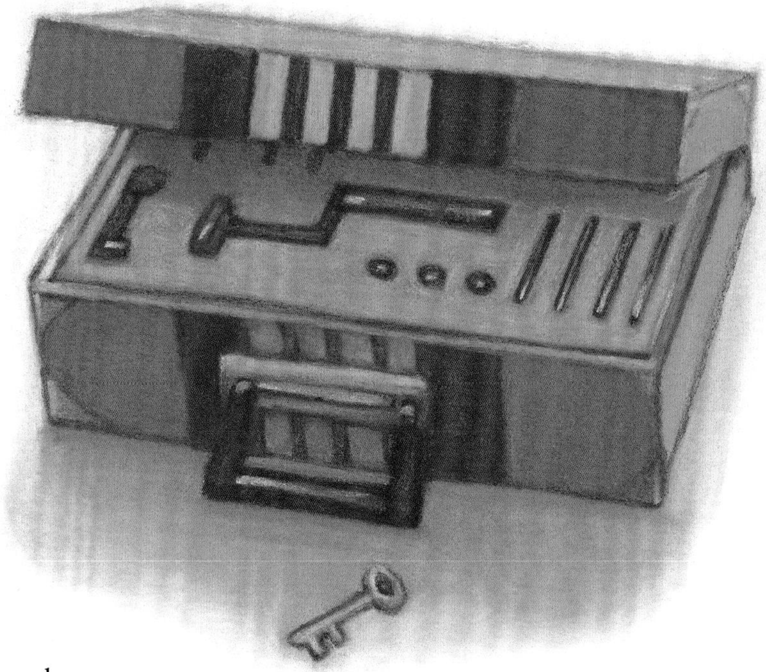

In half an hour Jimmy went down stairs and through the cafe. He was now dressed in tasteful and well-fitting clothes, and carried his dusted and cleaned suitcase in his hand. "Got anything on?" asked Mike Dolan, genially.

"Me?" said Jimmy, in a puzzled tone. "I don't understand. I'm representing the New York Amalgamated Short Snap Biscuit Cracker and Frazzled Wheat Company."

This statement delighted Mike to such an extent that Jimmy had to take a seltzer-and-milk on the spot. He never touched "hard" drinks.

representing—*as a traveling salesman*
"hard"—*alcoholic*

A week after the release of Valentine, 9762, there was a neat job of safe burglary done in Richmond, Indiana, with no clue to the author. A scant eight hundred dollars was all that was secured. Two weeks after that a patented, improved, burglar-proof safe in Logansport was opened like a cheese to the tune of fifteen hundred dollars, currency; securities and silver untouched. That began to interest the rogue catchers. Then an old-fashioned bank-safe in Jefferson City became active and threw out of its crater an eruption of bank-notes amounting to five thousand dollars. The losses were now high enough to bring the matter up into Ben Price's class of work. By comparing notes, a remarkable similarity in the methods of the burglaries was noticed.

Ben Price investigated the scenes of the robberies, and was heard to remark: "That's Dandy Jim Valentine's autograph. He's resumed business. Look at that combination knob — jerked out as easy as pulling up a radish in wet weather. He's got the only clamps that can do it. And look how clean those tumblers were punched out! Jimmy never has to drill but one hole. Yes, I guess I want Mr. Valentine. He'll do his bit next time without any short-time or clemency foolishness."

rogue catchers—*detectives*
combination knob—*on the lock of the safe*
tumblers—*in the lock mechanism*
short-time or clemency—*shortened prison sentence, or immediate release*

Ben Price knew Jimmy's habits. He had learned them while working on the Springfield case. Long jumps, quick get-aways, no confederates, and a taste for good society—these ways had helped Mr. Valentine to become noted as a successful dodger of retribution. It was given out that Ben Price had taken up the trail of the elusive cracksman, and other people with burglar-proof safes felt more at ease.

One afternoon Jimmy Valentine and his suitcase climbed out of the mail-hack in Elmore, a little town five miles off the railroad down in the blackjack country of Arkansas. Jimmy, looking like an athletic young senior just home from college, went down the board side-walk toward the hotel.

A young lady crossed the street, passed him at the corner and entered a door over which was the sign, "The Elmore Bank." Jimmy Valentine looked into her eyes, forgot what he was, and became another man. She lowered her eyes and colored slightly. Young men of Jimmy's style and looks were scarce in Elmore.

Jimmy collared a boy that was loafing on the steps of the bank as if he were one of the stockholders, and began to ask him questions about the town, feeding him dimes at intervals. By and by the young lady came out, looking royally unconscious of the young man with the suit-case, and went her way.

"Isn' that young lady Polly Simpson?" asked Jimmy, with specious guile.

"Naw," said the boy. "She's Annabel Adams. Her pa owns this bank. Why'd you come to Elmore for? Is that a gold watch chain? I'm going to get a bulldog. Got any more dimes?"

Jimmy went to the Planters' Hotel, registered as Ralph D. Spencer, and engaged a room. He leaned on the desk and declared his platform to the clerk. He said he had come to Elmore to look for a location to go into business. How was the shoe business, now, in the town? He had thought of the shoe business. Was there an opening?

The clerk was impressed by the clothes and manner of Jimmy. He, himself,

confederates—*partners in crime*
specious guile—*deceptive craftiness*

was something of a pattern of fashion to the thinly gilded youth of Elmore, but he now perceived his shortcomings. While trying to figure out Jimmy's manner of tying his four-in-hand he cordially gave information.

Yes, there ought to be a good opening in the shoe line. There wasn't an exclusive shoe-store in the place. The dry goods and general stores handled them. Business in all lines was fairly good. Hoped Mr. Spencer would decide to locate in Elmore. He would find it a pleasant town to live in, and the people very sociable.

Mr. Spencer thought he would stop over in the town a few days and look over the situation. No, the clerk needn't call the boy. He would carry up his suitcase, himself; it was rather heavy.

Mr. Ralph Spencer, the phoenix that arose from Jimmy Valentine's ashes—ashes left by the flame of a sudden and alterative attack of love—remained in Elmore, and prospered. He opened a shoe-store and secured a good run of trade.

Socially he was also a success, and made many friends. And he accomplished the wish of his heart. He met Miss Annabel Adams, and became more and more captivated by her charms.

At the end of a year the situation of Mr. Ralph Spencer was this: he had won the respect of the community, his shoe store was flourishing, and he and Annabel were engaged to be married in two weeks. Mr. Adams, the typical, plodding, country banker, approved of Spencer. Annabel's pride in him almost equalled her affection. He was as much at home in the family of Mr. Adams and that of Annabel's married sister as if he were already a member.

pattern—*figure*
thinly gilded youth—*not too rich or fashionable*
four-in-hand—*necktie*
dry goods—*clothing and fabric*
phoenix— *a mythical bird; it lives for a hundred years, then bursts into flames and completely burns up; then out of its ashes, a new phoenix arises*
alterative— *producing changes of physical feelings*

One day Jimmy sat down in his room and wrote this letter, which he mailed to the safe address of one of his old friends in St. Louis:

Dear Old Pal: I want you to be at Sullivan's place, in Little Rock, next Wednesday night, at nine o'clock. I want you to wind up some little matters for me. And, also, I want to make you a present of my kit of tools. I know you'll be glad to get them—you couldn't duplicate the lot for a thousand dollars. Say, Billy, I've quit the old business—a year ago. I've got a nice store. I'm making an honest living, and I'm going to marry the finest girl on earth two weeks from now. It's the only life, Billy—the straight one. I wouldn't touch a dollar of another man's money now for a million.

After I get married I'm going to sell out and go West, where there won't be so much danger of having old scores brought up against me. I tell you, Billy, she's an angel. She believes in me; and I wouldn't do another crooked thing for the whole world. Be sure to be at Sully's, for I must see you. I'll bring along the tools with me.

Your old friend, Jimmy.

On the Monday night after Jimmy wrote this letter, Ben Price jogged unobtrusively into Elmore in a livery buggy. He lounged about town in his quiet way until he found out what he wanted to know. From the drug-store across the street from Spencer's shoe store he got a good look at Ralph D. Spencer.

"Going to marry the banker's daughter are you, Jimmy?" said Ben to himself, softly. "Well, I don't know!"

The next morning Jimmy took breakfast at the Adamses. He was going to Little Rock that day to order his wedding suit and buy something nice for Annabel. That would be the first time he had left town since he came to Elmore. It had been more than a year now since those last professional "jobs," and he thought he could safely venture out.

After breakfast quite a family party went downtown together—Mr. Adams, Annabel, Jimmy, and Annabel's married sister with her two little girls, aged five

livery buggy—*rented horse-drawn carriage*

and nine. They came by the hotel where Jimmy still boarded, and he ran up to his room and brought along his suitcase. Then they went on to the bank. There stood Jimmy's horse and buggy and Dolph Gibson, who was going to drive him over to the railroad station.

All went inside the high, carved oak railings into the banking room—Jimmy included, for Mr. Adams's future son-in-law was welcome anywhere. The clerks were pleased to be greeted by the good-looking, agreeable young man who was going to marry Miss Annabel. Jimmy set his suitcase down. Annabel, whose heart was bubbling with happiness and lively youth, put on Jimmy's hat, and picked up the suitcase.

"Wouldn't I make a nice drummer?" said Annabel. "My! Ralph, how heavy it is? Feels like it was full of gold bricks."

"Lot of nickel-plated shoehorns in there," said Jimmy, coolly, "that I'm going to return. Thought I'd save express charges by taking them up. I'm getting awfully economical."

The Elmore Bank had just put in a new safe and vault. Mr. Adams was very proud of it, and insisted on an inspection by every one. The vault was a small one, but it had a new, patented door. It fastened with three solid steel bolts thrown simultaneously with a single handle, and had a time lock. Mr. Adams beamingly explained its workings to Mr. Spencer, who showed a courteous but not too intelligent interest. The two children, May and Agatha, were delighted by the shining metal and funny clock and knobs.

While they were thus engaged Ben Price sauntered in and leaned on his elbow, looking casually inside between the railings. He told the teller that he didn't want anything; he was just waiting for a man he knew.

Suddenly there was a scream or two from the women, and a commotion. Unperceived by the elders, May, the nine-year-old girl, in a spirit of play, had shut Agatha in the vault. She had then shot the bolts and turned the knob of the combination as she had seen Mr. Adams do.

drummer—*traveling salesman, with a heavy case of samples*

The old banker sprang to the handle and tugged at it for a moment.

"The door can't be opened," he groaned. "The clock hasn't been wound nor the combination set."

Agatha's mother screamed again, hysterically.

"Hush!" said Mr. Adams, raising his trembling hand. "All be quite for a moment. Agatha!" he called as loudly as he could. "Listen to me."

During the following silence they could just hear the faint sound of the child wildly shrieking in the dark vault in a panic of terror.

"My precious darling!" wailed the mother. "She will die of fright!

Open the door! Oh, break it open! Can't you men do something?"

"There isn't a man nearer than Little Rock who can open that door," said Mr. Adams, in a shaky voice. "My God! Spencer, what shall we do? That child—she can't stand it long in there. There isn't enough air, and, besides, she'll go into convulsions from fright."

Agatha's mother, frantic now, beat the door of the vault with her hands. Somebody wildly suggested dynamite. Annabel turned to Jimmy, her large eyes full of anguish, but not yet despairing. To a woman nothing seems quite impossible to the powers of the man she worships.

"Can't you do something, Ralph—try, won't you?"

He looked at her with a queer, soft smile on his lips and in his keen eyes.

convulsions—*fits*

"Annabel," he said, "give me that rose you are wearing, will you?"

Hardly believing that she heard him aright, she unpinned the bud from the bosom of her dress, and placed it in his hand. Jimmy stuffed it into his vest-pocket, threw off his coat and pulled up his shirt- sleeves. With that act Ralph D. Spencer passed away and Jimmy Valentine took his place.

"Get away from the door, all of you," he commanded, shortly.

He set his suitcase on the table, and opened it out flat. From that time on he seemed to be unconscious of the presence of anyone else.

He laid out the shining, queer implements swiftly and orderly, whistling softly to himself as he always did when at work. In a deep silence and immovable, the others watched him as if under a spell.

In a minute Jimmy's pet drill was biting smoothly into the steel door.

In ten minutes—breaking his own burglarious record—he threw back the bolts and opened the door.

Agatha, almost collapsed, but safe, was gathered into her mother's arms.

Jimmy Valentine put on his coat, and walked outside the railings towards the front door. As he went he thought he heard a far-away voice that he once knew call "Ralph!" But he never hesitated.

At the door a big man stood somewhat in his way.

"Hello, Ben!" said Jimmy, still with his strange smile. "Got around at last, have you? Well, let's go. I don't know that it makes much difference, now."

And then Ben Price acted rather strangely.

"Guess you're mistaken, Mr. Spencer," he said. "Don't believe I recognize you. Your buggy's waiting for you, ain't it?"

And Ben Price turned and strolled down the street.

implements—*tools*

THE PIMIENTA PANCAKES

1907

This is one of many stories by O. Henry about the American West, where he lived as a young man before moving to New York and becoming widely known as a writer. It is told by a narrator about Jud Odom, the cook on a cattle ranch. But the real tale is a story-within-a-story, which Jud tells about himself, an attractive young lady, and a sheep rancher named Jackson Bird. There was an ongoing conflict in that part of the country between those who raised cattle and sheep. The "Pimienta Crossing" is a fictional spot, but it is set in an actual location in south-central Texas, in the country between the Nueces and Frio rivers, near where O. Henry first lived on a ranch before he moved to Austin.

In this story, both Jud and the narrator use language that is an amusing blend of the fancy talk of well-read people and the straight talk of frontier cowboys. For example, Jud reports first seeing Willella as "an imported girl with fixings on" (meaning fancy clothes), but then says jokingly that she is "philandering" with a croquet mallet ("philandering" usually means a fickle man's flirtations with women). "The Pimienta Pancakes" is comically amusing in a different way from the other stories in this book. The tone is set by the way Jud talks in a story he tells against himself. Is the irony in the story any different because of this?

WHILE WE WERE ROUNDING UP A BUNCH OF THE Triangle-O cattle in the Frio bottoms, a projecting branch of a dead mesquite caught my wooden stirrup and gave my ankle a wrench that laid me up in camp for a week.

On the third day of my compulsory idleness I crawled out near the grub wagon, and reclined helpless under the conversational fire of Judson Odom, the camp cook. Jud was a monologist by nature, whom Destiny, with customary blundering, had set in a profession wherein he was bereaved, for the greater portion of his time, of an audience.

Therefore, I was manna in the desert of Jud's obmutescence. Betimes I was stirred by invalid longings for something to eat that did not come under the caption of "grub." I had visions of the maternal pantry "deep as first love, and wild with all regret," and then I asked: "Jud, can you make pancakes?"

Jud laid down his six-shooter, with which he was preparing to pound an antelope steak, and stood over me in what I felt to be a menacing attitude. He further endorsed my impression that his pose was resentful by fixing upon me with his light blue eyes a look of cold suspicion.

"Say, you," he said, with candid, though not excessive, choler, "did you mean that straight, or was you trying to throw the gaff into me?

Some of the boys been telling you about me and that pancake racket?"

"No, Jud," I said, sincerely, "I meant it. It seems to me I'd swap my pony

Triangle-O—*the name of a ranch*
Frio bottoms—*low-lying land along the river in southern Texas*
monologist—*solo theatrical performer*
profession wherein he was bereaved, for the greater portion of his time, of an audience—*because he worked alone in the kitchen, there were seldom people around to listen*
manna in the desert—*in the Bible, food that dropped from Heaven to feed the wandering Israelites in the desert*
obmutescence—*remaining speechless*
choler—*anger*

and saddle for a stack of buttered brown pancakes with some first crop, open kettle, New Orleans sweetening. Was there a story about pancakes?"

Jud was mollified at once when he saw that I had not been dealing in allusions. He brought some mysterious bags and tin boxes from the grub wagon and set them in the shade of the hackberry where I lay reclined. I watched him as he began to arrange them leisurely and untie their many strings.

"No, not a story," said Jud, as he worked, "but just the logical disclosures in the case of me and that pink-eyed snoozer from Mired Mule Canada and Miss Willella Learight. I don't mind telling you.

"I was punching then for old Bill Toomey, on the San Miguel. One day I gets all ensnared up in aspirations for to eat some canned grub that hasn't ever mooed or baaed or grunted or been in peck measures. So, I gets on my bronc and pushes the wind for Uncle Emsley Telfair's store at the Pimienta Crossing on the Nueces.

"About three in the afternoon I throwed my bridle rein over a mesquite limb and walked the last twenty yards into Uncle Emsley's store. I got up on the counter and told Uncle Emsley that the signs pointed to the devastation of the fruit crop of the world. In a minute I had a bag of crackers and a long-handled spoon, with an open can each of apricots and pineapples and cherries and greengages beside of me with Uncle Emsley busy chopping away with the hatchet at the yellow clings. I was feeling like Adam before the apple stampede, and was digging my spurs into the side of the counter and working with my

mollified—*relieved*
dealing in allusions—*joking with him about the pancakes*
punching—*herding cattle*
peck measures—*like grain*
Nueces—*river in southern Texas*
yellow clings—*peaches*

twenty-four-inch spoon when I happened to look out of the window into the yard of Uncle Emsley's house, which was next to the store.

"There was a girl standing there — an imported girl with fixings on — philandering with a croquet maul and amusing herself by watching my style of encouraging the fruit canning industry.

"I slid off the counter and delivered up my shovel to Uncle Emsley.

"'That's my niece,' says he; 'Miss Willella Learight, down from Palestine on a visit. Do you want that I should make you acquainteds'?

"'The Holy Land,' I says to myself, my thoughts milling some as I tried to run 'em into the corral. 'Why not? There was sure angels in Pales—Why, yes, Uncle Emsley,' I says out loud, 'I'd be awful edified to meet Miss Learight.' So Uncle Emsley took me out in the yard and gave us each other's entitlements...

"I never was shy about women. I never could understand why some men who can break a mustang before breakfast and shave in the dark, get all left-handed and full of perspiration and excuses when they see a bolt of calico draped around what belongs to it. Inside of eight minutes me and Miss Willella was aggravating the croquet balls around as amiable as

philandering—*playing around with*
maul—*mallet*
Palestine—*town three hundred miles to the north*
edified—*instructed so as to be improved*
gave us each other's entitlements—*introduced us*
calico—*cloth with bright-colored designs*

second cousins. She gave me a dig about the quantity of canned fruit I had eaten, and I got back at her, flat-footed, about how a certain lady named Eve started the fruit trouble in the first free-grass pasture—'Over in Palestine, wasn't it?' says I, as easy and pat as roping a one-year-old.

"That was how I acquired cordiality for the proximities of Miss Willella Learight; and the disposition grew larger as time passed. She was stopping at Pimienta Crossing for her health, which was very good, and for the climate, which was forty percent. hotter than Palestine. I rode over to see her once every week for a while; and then I figured it out that if I doubled the number of trips I would see her twice as often.

"One week I slipped in a third trip; and that's where the pancakes and the pink-eyed snoozer busted into the game.

"That evening, while I set on the counter with a peach and two damsons in my mouth, I asked Uncle Emsley how Miss Willella was.

"'Why,' says Uncle Emsley, 'she's gone riding with Jackson Bird, the sheep man from over at Mired Mule Canada.' I swallowed the peach seed and the two damson seeds. I guess somebody held the counter by the bridle while I got off; and then I walked out straight ahead till I butted against the mesquite where my roan was tied.

"'She's gone riding,' I whisper in my bronc's ear, 'with Birdstone Jack, the hired mule from Sheep Man's Canada. Did you get that, old Leather-and-Gallops?' "That bronc of mine wept, in his way. He'd been raised a cow pony and he didn't care for snoozers.

"I went back and said to Uncle Emsley: 'Did you say a sheep man?'

" 'I said a sheep man,' says Uncle Emsley again. 'You must have heard tell of Jackson Bird. He's got eight sections of grazing and four thousand head of the finest Merinos south of the Arctic Circle.'

"I went out and sat on the ground in the shade of the store and leaned against a prickly pear. I sifted sand into my boots with unthinking

aggravating—*upsetting, distressing*
cordiality for the proximities—*came to like being around her*
roan—*red horse*
bronc's—*horse's*
Merinos—*kind of sheep*

hands while I soliloquised a quantity about this bird with the Jackson plumage to his name.

"I never had believed in harming sheep men. I see one, one day, reading a Latin grammar on hossback, and I never touched him! They never irritated me like they do most cowmen. You wouldn't go to work now, and impair and disfigure snoozers, would you, that eat on tables and wear little shoes and speak to you on subjects? I had always let 'em pass, just as you would a jack rabbit; with a polite word and a guess about the weather, but no stopping to swap canteens. I never thought it was worth while to be hostile with a snoozer. And because I'd been lenient, and let 'em live, here was one going around riding with Miss Willella Learight!

"An hour by sun they come loping back, and stopped at Uncle Emsley's gate. The sheep person helped her off; and they stood throwing each other sentences all sprightful and sagacious for a while. And then this feathered Jackson flies up

soliloquised—*talked to myself*
impair and disfigure—*belittle and bully*
sprightful—*lively*
sagacious—*wise*

in his saddle and raises his little stewpot of a hat, and trots off in the direction of his mutton ranch.

"By this time I had turned the sand out of my boots and unpinned myself from the prickly pear; and by the time he gets half a mile out of Pimienta, I singlefoots up beside him on my bronc.

"I said that snoozer was pink-eyed, but he wasn't. His seeing arrangement was grey enough, but his eye-lashes was pink and his hair was sandy, and that gave you the idea. Sheep man?—he wasn't more than a lamb man, anyhow—a little thing with his neck involved in a yellow silk handkerchief, and shoes tied up in bowknots.

"'Afternoon!' says I to him. 'You now ride with a equestrian who is commonly called Dead-Moral-Certainty Judson, on account of the way I shoot. When I want a stranger to know me I always introduce myself before the draw, for I never did like to shake hands with ghosts.'

"'Ah,' says he, just like that—'Ah, I'm glad to know you, Mr. Judson. I'm Jackson Bird, from over at Mired Mule Ranch.' Just then one of my eyes saw a roadrunner skipping down the hill with a young tarantula in his bill, and the other eye noticed a rabbit-hawk sitting on a dead limb in a water-elm. I popped over one after the other with my forty-five, just to show him. 'Two out of three,' says I. 'Birds just naturally seem to draw my fire wherever I go.'

"'Nice shooting,' says the sheep man, without a flutter. 'But don't you sometimes ever miss the third shot? Elegant fine rain that was last week for the young grass, Mr. Judson?' says he.

"'Willie,' says I, riding over close to his palfrey, 'your infatuated parents may have denounced you by the name of Jackson, but you sure moulted into a twittering Willie—let us slough off this here analysis of rain and the elements, and get down to talk that is outside the vocabulary of parrots. That is a bad habit you have got of riding with young ladies over at Pimienta. I've known birds,' says I, 'to be served on toast for less than that. Miss Willella,' says I, 'don't ever want

singlefoots—*a horse's pace between walking and trotting*
equestrian—*horseback rider*
tarantula—*large spider*
forty-five—*a six-shooter favored by cowboys*
moulted—*lost one's feathers, shrank*

any nest made out of sheep's wool by a tomtit of the Jacksonian branch of ornithology. Now, are you going to quit, or do you wish for to gallop up against this Dead-Moral-Certainty attachment to my name, which is good for two hyphens and at least one set of funeral obsequies?'

"Jackson Bird flushed up some, and then he laughed.

"'Why, Mr. Judson,' says he, 'you've got the wrong idea. I've called on Miss Learight a few times; but not for the purpose you imagine. My object is purely a gastronomical one.'

"I reached for my gun.

"'Any coyote,' says I, 'that would boast of dishonourable—'

"'Wait a minute,' says this Bird, 'till I explain. What would I do with a wife? If you ever saw that ranch of mine! I do my own cooking and mending. Eating—that's all the pleasure I get out of sheep raising. Mr. Judson, did you ever taste the pancakes that Miss Learight makes?'

"'Me? No,' I told him. 'I never was advised that she was up to any culinary manoeuvres.'

"'They're golden sunshine,' says he, 'honey-browned by the ambrosial fires of Epicurus. I'd give two years of my life to get the recipe for making

tomtit—*small bird*
ornithology—*the science of birds*
obsequies—*ceremonies*
gastronomical—*having to do with food one.*
culinary manoeuvres—*skillful sorts of cooking*
ambrosial fires of Epicurus.—*ambrosia was the food of the Greek gods; Epicurus was a Greek philosopher usually and mistakenly spoken of as recommending pleasure above all else: this is a comically fancy way of saying "browned in the oven"*

them pancakes. That's what I went to see Miss Learight for,' says Jackson Bird, 'but I haven't been able to get it from her. It's an old recipe that's been in the family for seventy-five years. They hand it down from one generation to another, but they don't give it away to outsiders. If I could get that recipe, so I could make them pancakes for myself on my ranch, I'd be a happy man,' says Bird.

"'Are you sure,' I says to him, 'that it ain't the hand that mixes the pancakes that you're after?'

"'Sure,' says Jackson. 'Miss Learight is a mighty nice girl, but I can assure you my intentions go no further than the gastro—' but he seen my hand going down to my holster and he changed his similitude—'than the desire to procure a copy of the pancake recipe,' he finishes.

"'You ain't such a bad little man,' says I, trying to be fair. 'I was thinking some of making orphans of your sheep, but I'll let you fly away this time. But you stick to pancakes,' says I, 'as close as the middle one of a stack; and don't go and mistake sentiments for syrup, or there'll be singing at your ranch, and you won't hear it.'

"'To convince you that I am sincere,' says the sheep man, 'I'll ask you to help me. Miss Learight and you being closer friends, maybe she would do for you what she wouldn't for me. If you will get me a copy of that pancake recipe, I give you my word that I'll never call upon her again.'

"'That's fair,' I says, and I shook

gastro— *he starts to say "gastronomical"*
similitude—*comparison*

hands with Jackson Bird. 'I'll get it for you if I can, and glad to oblige.' And he turned off down the big pear flat on the Piedra, in the direction of Mired Mule; and I steered northwest for old Bill Toomey's ranch.

"It was five days afterward when I got another chance to ride over to Pimienta. Miss Willella and me passed a gratifying evening at Uncle Emsley's. She sang some, and exasperated the piano quite a lot with quotations from the operas. I gave imitations of a rattlesnake, and told her about Snaky McFee's new way of skinning cows, and described the trip I made to Saint Louis once. We was getting along in one another's estimations fine. Thinks I, if Jackson Bird can now be persuaded to migrate, I win. I recollect his promise about the pancake receipt, and I thinks I will persuade it from Miss Willella and give it to him; and then if I catches Birdie off of Mired Mule again, I'll make him hop the twig.

"So, along about ten o'clock, I put on a wheedling smile and says to Miss Willella: 'Now, if there's anything I do like better than the sight of a red steer on green grass it's the taste of a nice hot pancake smothered in sugar-house molasses.'

"Miss Willella gives a little jump on the piano stool, and looked at me curious.

"'Yes,' says she, 'they're real nice. What did you say was the name of that street in Saint Louis, Mr. Odom, where you lost your hat?'

"'Pancake Avenue,' says I, with a wink, to show her that I was on about the family receipt, and couldn't be side-corralled off of the subject. 'Come, now, Miss Willella,' I says; 'let's hear how you make 'em. Pancakes is just whirling in my head like wagon wheels. Start her off, now—pound of flour, eight dozen eggs, and so on. How does the catalogue of constituents run?'

"'Excuse me for a moment, please,' says Miss Willella, and she gives me a quick kind of sideways look, and slides off the stool. She ambled out into the other room, and directly Uncle Emsley comes in in his shirtsleeves, with a pitcher of water. He turns around to get a glass on the table, and I see a forty-five in his hip pocket. 'Great post- holes!' thinks I,

hop the twig—*buzz off; run away*
constituents—*ingredients*

'but here's a family thinks a heap of cooking receipts, protecting it with firearms. I've known outfits that wouldn't do that much by a family feud.'

"'Drink this here down,' says Uncle Emsley, handing me the glass of water. 'You've rid too far today, Jud, and got yourself overexcited. Try to think about something else now.'

"'Do you know how to make them pancakes, Uncle Emsley?' I asked.

"'Well, I'm not as apprised in the anatomy of them as some,' says Uncle Emsley, 'but I reckon you take a sifter of plaster of Paris and a little dough and saleratus and corn meal, and mix 'em with eggs and buttermilk as usual. Is old Bill going to ship beeves to Kansas City again this spring, Jud?'

"That was all the pancake specifications I could get that night. I didn't wonder that Jackson Bird found it uphill work. So I dropped the subject and talked with Uncle Emsley for a while about hollow horn and cyclones. And then Miss Willella came and said 'Good-night,' and I hit the breeze for the ranch.

"About a week afterward I met Jackson Bird riding out of Pimienta as I rode in, and we stopped on the road for a few frivolous remarks.

"'Got the bill of particulars for them flapjacks yet?' I asked him.

"'Well, no,' says Jackson. 'I don't seem to have any success in getting hold of it. Did you try?'

"'I did,' says I, 'and 'twas like trying to dig a prairie dog out of his hole with a peanut hull. That pancake receipt must be a jookalorum, the way they hold on to it.'

receipts—*recipes*
plaster of Paris—*a quick setting white powder used to cast statues*
saleratus—*baking powder or soda*
jookalorum—*really something*

"'I'm most ready to give it up,' says Jackson, so discouraged in his pronunciations that I felt sorry for him; 'but I did want to know how to make them pancakes to eat on my lonely ranch,' says he. 'I lie awake at nights thinking how good they are.'

"'You keep on trying for it,' I tells him, 'and I'll do the same. One of us is bound to get a rope over its horns before long. Well, so long, Jacksy.'

"You see, by this time we were on the peacefullest of terms. When I saw that he wasn't after Miss Willella, I had more endurable contemplations of that sandy-haired snoozer. In order to help out the ambitions of his appetite I kept on trying to get that receipt from Miss Willella. But every time I would say 'pancakes' she would get sort of remote and fidgety about the eye, and try to change the subject. If I held her to it she would slide out and round up Uncle Emsley with his pitcher of water and hip-pocket howitzer.

"One day I galloped over to the store with a fine bunch of blue verbenas that I cut out of a herd of wild flowers over on Poisoned Dog Prairie. Uncle Emsley looked at 'em with one eye shut and says: 'Haven't ye heard the news?'

"'Cattle up?' I asks.

"'Willella and Jackson Bird was married in Palestine yesterday,' says he. 'Just got a letter this morning.'

"I dropped them flowers in a cracker-barrel, and let the news trickle in my ears and down toward my upper left-hand shirt pocket until it got to my feet.

"'Would you mind saying that over again once more, Uncle Emsley?' says I. 'Maybe my hearing has got wrong, and you only said that prime heifers was four-eighty on the hoof, or something like that.'

"'Married yesterday,' says Uncle Emsley, 'and gone to Waco and Niagara Falls on a wedding tour. Why, didn't you see none of the signs all along? Jackson Bird has been courting Willella ever since that day he took her out riding.'

"'Then,' says I, in a kind of yell, 'what was all this zizzaparoola he gives me about pancakes? Tell me that.'

pronunciations—*pronouncements*
snoozer—*guy, fella*
hip-pocket howitzer—*comic for "revolver," a howitzer was a large cannon*
four-eighty on the hoof—*market price*
zizzaparoola—*comic word for "nonsense"*

"When I said 'pancakes' Uncle Emsley sort of dodged and stepped back.

"'Somebody's been dealing me pancakes from the bottom of the deck,' I says, 'and I'll find out. I believe you know. Talk up,' says I, 'or we'll mix a panful of batter right here.'

"I slid over the counter after Uncle Emsley. He grabbed at his gun, but it was in a drawer, and he missed it by two inches. I got him by the front of his shirt and shoved him in a corner.

"'Talk pancakes,' says I, 'or be made into one. Does Miss Willella make 'em?'

"'She never made one in her life and I never saw one,' says Uncle Emsley, soothing. 'Calm down now, Jud—calm down. You've got excited, and that wound in your head is contaminating your sense of intelligence. Try not to think about pancakes.'

"'Uncle Emsley,' says I, 'I'm not wounded in the head except so far as my natural cognitive instincts run to runts. Jackson Bird told me he was calling on Miss Willella for the purpose of finding out her system of producing pancakes, and he asked me to help him get the bill of lading of the ingredients. I done so, with the results as you see. Have I been sodded down with Johnson grass by a pink-eyed snoozer, or what?'

"'Slack up your grip in my dress shirt,' says Uncle Emsley, 'and I'll tell you. Yes, it looks like Jackson Bird has gone and humbugged you some. The day after he went riding with Willella he came back and told me and her to watch out for you whenever you got to talking about pancakes. He said you was in camp once where they was cooking flapjacks, and one

contaminating—*gloss?*
bill of lading—*receipt for shipped goods*
sodded down—*bloated*
Johnson grass—*grass cultivated for feeding cattle and horses*

of the fellows cut you over the head with a frying pan. Jackson said that whenever you got overhot or excited that wound hurt you and made you kind of crazy, and you went raving about pancakes. He told us to just get you worked off of the subject and soothed down, and you wouldn't be dangerous. So, me and Willella done the best by you we knew how. Well, well,' says Uncle Emsley, 'that Jackson Bird is sure a seldom kind of a snoozer.'"

During the progress of Jud's story he had been slowly but deftly combining certain portions of the contents of his sacks and cans.

Toward the close of it he set before me the finished product—a pair of red-hot, rich-hued pancakes on a tin plate. From some secret hoarding he also brought a lump of excellent butter and a bottle of golden syrup.

"How long ago did these things happen?" I asked him.

"Three years," said Jud. "They're living on the Mired Mule Ranch now. But I haven't seen either of 'em since. They say Jackson Bird was fixing his ranch up fine with rocking chairs and window curtains all the time he was putting me up the pancake tree. Oh, I got over it after a while. But the boys kept the racket up."

"Did you make these cakes by the famous recipe?" I asked.

"Didn't I tell you there wasn't no receipt?" said Jud. "The boys hollered pancakes till they got pancake hungry, and I cut this recipe out of a newspaper. How does the truck taste?"

"They're delicious," I answered. "Why don't you have some, too, Jud?"

I was sure I heard a sigh.

"Me?" said Jud. "I don't ever eat 'em."

deftly—*quickly and skillfully*